A
FAST
AND
BRUTAL
WING

Also by Kathleen Jeffrie Johnson

TARGET

The
Parallel
Universe
of Liars

Kathleen Jeffrie Johnson

A FAST AND BRUTAL WING

 A Deborah Brodie Book   Roaring Brook Press   Brookfield, Connecticut seedcake for my rainbow actor,

my handed crow.

always.

Copyright © 2004 by Kathleen Jeffrie Johnson

A Deborah Brodie Book
Published by Roaring Brook Press
A Division of Holtzbrinck Publishing Holdings Limited Partnership
2 Old New Milford Road
Brookfield, Connecticut 06804

Library of Congress Cataloging-in-Publication Data on file

ISBN 1-59643-013-3

10 9 8 7 6 5 4 3 2 1

Book design by Jaye Zimet
Printed in the United States of America

First edition

Emmet Marcona
Tomington Center—Wing A—Dr. Milton
Assignment
November 5

Why do you want me to write down what happened?
I know I don't talk much—but that's because I'm a
quiet person. There's nothing wrong with that.

Here's what happened: Nothing.

I went for a walk in the woods on Halloween with Niki
and Doug, and Doug got scared. Maybe we shouldn't
have gone there at night, but really, that's all it
was. It's true that Niki and I got in a fight and
yelled at each other. Doug doesn't have any
siblings, though, and doesn't understand, so he
panicked and called the police.

I feel terrible that Niki is upset. Why won't you let
me call her? Despite our differences, we've always
had a connection. Just like all brothers and sisters, I
mean. I don't want her to think badly of me.

You asked me what she's like. Well, she's just—Niki.

It's true she's a little bit crazy. Kind of a pisser.
Younger than me by two years, but always bossing
me around, acting like she's older by centuries.
She's always been that way—strong in a way I'm
not. And she's got this wild imagination, pretending

we belong to another world, all caught up in fantasy.

Listen, she keeps a hard edge, so no one will know how soft she is inside, but I know. So don't get all psyched out by her. She's like a little kid, really, the way she still believes in magic. And this is her favorite fantasy of all—animals changing into people, people changing into animals. She calls it transformation. As if there's this whole other world just waiting, if only we'd open ourselves up.

She likes to write, so I told her to write down one of her stories for the Father Project at school. I thought maybe it would help her work Dad out of her system—put him into a fantasy and either bring him back or kill him off.

It was a mistake, I guess. I haven't read her story—she wouldn't let me—but I can see that focusing on our father probably made things worse.

This is typical: One night, while Mom made dinner, I stood in the doorway to the living room, watching Niki push and shove all the throw pillows on the couch into a comfy mound, then curl up against them like a cat and fall asleep. She wants to be a cat, but she isn't, and she knows it. It's just a game she plays. Look, she can fall asleep like no one I know. Or stay wide awake forever, watching.

She watches me, what I'm up to. Except I'm not up to

anything. I go to school. I take long walks in the woods that start behind our home and stretch all the way past Doug Bracken's place, where the forest is thick and fat. Sometimes I pass the old house where that crazy writer lives. Every so often I see him peering out a window, watching me, but I just blend back into the trees until I'm alone again. That's what I like best: being alone.

As for Dad, two years ago he ran off with another woman—I guess you know that by now, though. Original, huh? So Mom said I had to be a responsible older brother to Niki. But I knew she meant father.

I'm not father material, though. Not even older brother material. I want to leave, really. Go off on my own.

But I'm obviously not going anywhere. Not while I'm stuck here at Tomington—for no reason that I can figure. Maybe I'm not talking much, but that's not exactly a crime. I know I'm not crazy. And look—my fingers are doing all right with this pencil. They work just fine. I'm human like everybody else.

How much longer will I be here? I want to go home.

From: Douglas Bracken <dougman@minimen.com>
To: Dr. Rita I. Milton <Milton@tellet.com>
Sent: Wednesday, November 06—4:26 PM
Subject: HI, IT'S ME!!!!!!

Dr. Milton,

So--you want me to write out everything that happened, like an official report or something? I can do that!

I'm glad e-mail is OK. I promise I'll use my best grammar and stuff. I'm no slumper! That's what my English teacher calls someone who sends him an e-mail in chatspeak, using a "u" for "you," or "ur" for "your." He prints it out and writes <u>Slumper!</u> in red ink right across the top of the page, then waves it in front of the class. And don't get him going about instant messaging! I agree with him that the e-mail style is probably destroying the English language. What's ur opinion? (Ha!)

Seriously, I'm a pretty good writer. I do great poems!

When Dad told me you called last night, I got a little nervous--I'd never heard from a psychiatrist before. I waited to answer until I felt, you know, <u>focused</u>. So when I got home today from school, I went for a walk in the woods. (Not where the police are nosing around. I stayed way clear of them--they don't know all the paths that I do.)

Is Emmet any better? Dad said you sounded nice, so I'm glad you're Emmet's shrink. And I'm happy someone finally wants to talk to me who thinks I'm human. Everybody else acts like I'm a weirdo whack-doodle <u>animal</u> of some kind. Is Emmet still not speaking? He wouldn't say one word after we left the woods that night, not even after the police came. And now nobody will let me know how he is. I can't even talk to Niki. (Mothers can be very protective of their young. Have you noticed?) Anyway, I wish Emmet wasn't being kept so far away, so I could visit. (You didn't call because you think I'm crazy, too, did you?)(?)

I heard on the news this morning that Chief Wilkinson plans to assign even more officers to search the part of the woods where everything happened. Maybe you could tell him that it isn't necessary? I've sent two e-mails already, explaining that nothing happened, but he hasn't responded. I mean, they won't find anything. I know I'm the one who called and made a report in the first place (dumb!) but I've since recanted. (Is that the right word?) I'm sure Mr. Slanger will turn up sooner or later. I've heard that eccentric writers often go missing. I mean, he was probably missing from somewhere else when he moved here. To be honest, he's kind of a snot. He's lived here for like 3 years and never once came to our school or offered to autograph my copy of his book--and tons of his fans are teens! (I loved BLOODWOLF.) As a writer myself, I'm sensitive to these things. I'd give everybody my autograph! Some people just shouldn't be allowed to become so famous.

I have to go start dinner. It's my turn to cook, and I like to have everything ready when Dad comes home--he's always hungry! Have you ever made scalloped potatoes? Not the kind in the box. The real thing. This is my second try. The first time, everything turned to mush, so wish me luck.

More later,
Doug Bracken
"Twenty pounds of spuds"

From: Douglas Bracken <dougman@minimen.com>
To: Dr. Rita I. Milton <Milton@tellet.com>
Sent: Thursday, November 07—5:02 PM
Subject: Re: Character Study

Dear Dr. Milton, hi.

No, I haven't read Niki's story. Not yet, anyway. She's very private, so I don't know if she'll let me read it or not. I told her she should write something for the Father Project at school, so I'm glad she listened to me—she doesn't necessarily do what you want her to. Did I mention that I write poetry?

I guess there's still no word on what happened to Mr. Slanger? I know I said he was attacked in the woods that night, but that's just silly. As I told the police, I knocked myself out by running into a tree branch (<u>major stupido!</u>) and when I came to, well, you know--dark night, wind, branches whipping around--spooky Halloween stuff! I was a total bongo brain. Maybe I hallucinated or something. If you hear anything from Chief Wilkinson, though, could you let me know? I think the police are a lot like Niki--tight-lipped.

I like Niki a lot! I mean, just as a friend. She's not like the other girls at school, who are just, you know, trying to be <u>hot</u> all the time. Niki's different, she belongs in a Viking poem or something. Maybe <u>Beowulf</u>. Not afraid to fight monsters. Especially since her father left.

Her mom's really nice. Maybe a little oblivious. (You won't tell her I said that, will you? Besides, with everything that's happened, she's probably on full Mom Alert by now.) I know all this stuff must be upsetting to her, with Emmet in the hospital and Niki home from school. And she's missing work! (Did you know Mrs. Marcona is a teacher? Fifth grade. My fifth-grade teacher's name was Mr. Bullet. I mean, really.) My mom would have stayed home with me, too, if she hadn't already been a stay-at-home mom. I broke my leg when I was nine, and she sat in my room and read stories to me for a whole week. That was before we moved out here. Did I mention that she died?

I just wish Mrs. Marcona hadn't had to see Niki and Emmet the way they were when we got out of the woods. You know.

Dad's still upset about what happened, but he shouldn't be, since nothing happened.

It's his turn to cook tonight. Usually he fixes hot dogs or fries up some sausage. He doesn't really understand the importance of vegetables.

All for now!
Doug Bracken
"Rutabagas are our friends"

It's Dr. Milton, right?—Emmet's doctor.
Mom told me what you want—the story I'm
writing for the Father Project. Well, too
bad, you can't have it. It isn't finished.

Besides, why should I give it to you?
You'll think it's merely fiction—but it's all
true.

I'm curious—why did you send a messenger
who looks like a weasel? He's so ugly. I have
to write this note with my back turned. You
should be more careful with the people you
hire.

Well, okay—maybe I'll give him a chapter.
Next time!

I told him to go eat a snake.

So when can Emmet come home? He isn't
crazy—you understand that, don't you? He's
simply being what he is. See, when you
transform, you don't become "Niki disguised
as a cat" or "Emmet acting like a hawk,
needing to be hospitalized." You become "cat"
or "hawk." Don't think it isn't possible.

It is.

Oh, all right. You can have Chapter 1.

Writer of Fantasy Missing

by CARL BRENNER
Mid-State News staff writer

GANTON—Police are still searching for Nicholas Slanger, missing since last Thursday from his home in Melville Co.

Late that evening, on Halloween, a local teenager placed a call to police stating that Mr. Slanger, the nationally acclaimed author of fantasy and horror, had been attacked by two of the teenager's friends in the woods that surround his home, just outside the city limits of Ganton. However, upon investigation, police found no evidence that Mr. Slanger had either been present or injured.

The two teenagers, though, were taken to a local hospital and treated for bites and scratches. One was released into the custody of family, the other was transferred to another medical facility.

The teenager who made the call later retracted his statement.

Chief Wilkinson commented, "While Mr. Slanger appears to be missing, we don't really know if a crime has been committed or not. He may simply have left the area. We are still investigating the altercation between the teenagers."

Slanger, the reclusive author of *Sky Hunt* and *Bloodwolf,* is known to have a reputation for eccentricity.

Because all the teenagers involved are minors, it is the policy of the *Mid-State News* not to publish their names.

THE FATHER PROJECT

Chapter One

Watching the hawk soar against the sky, its wings wide, the girl tried to dream herself into a bird. Almost, she could feel a fluffy down against her skin. Almost, she sensed the stiff prick of feathers. Almost, she felt the sprouting edge of wings, poking from her shoulder blades.

Almost.

"Honey, put on your jacket! You'll catch cold. Or come inside!"

N. turned away from the sky toward the back of their large, old, wood-frame house. Calling from a window on the second floor was her mother, her curly, dark hair glinting in the late afternoon sun. N. lifted her hand in response, and her mother slammed the window back down and disappeared.

N. shrugged. She wasn't cold. She wouldn't get cold until winter, when the temperatures really dropped. Now, in October, the air was cool and pleasant against her skin.

She searched out the hawk, found it circling high in the distance, probably above the thick patch of woods behind Doug Bracken's house. Her mother circled endlessly, too, watching her and Emmet—questioning, insisting, prying—but she saw nothing. Still, she was a better parent than their father—the Man Who Went Away. A mother fed you, offered you bits of meat to tempt your appetite. A father, though—what use was he? Hers was gone. Good.

Wait! The bird had disappeared. Darn. She'd been distracted again, by thoughts. She closed her eyes, imagining the hawk plunging soundlessly down through the sky, seizing a mouse or mole in its talons, and dragging it, shrieking, up toward the sun, small birds and crows screaming in protest.

She knew what would follow—irrevocable pain, the tearing of flesh, blood.

Loss.

She breathed deeply, almost tasting the broken animal in her mouth.

A breeze lifted her red-gold hair and she turned to walk toward the house. Dinner was in an hour. Emmet probably wouldn't be hungry. Her mother, upset, would complain about wasted food. But she knew nothing.

N. walked into the kitchen, hearing her mother's voice drifting down from the second floor, traveling the back stairway that ended in the kitchen. No doubt she was on her cell phone, talking to her sister, Aunt Tam. She was always talking to Aunt Tam, clinging to her words for advice and comfort. Aunt Tam explained all the things N.'s mother couldn't understand: The Man Who Went Away, her brother, N.

The warm, sickeningly sweet smell of cooked meat entered N.'s nose. She paused before the oven and opened it gingerly. Meatloaf, its juices spitting in the bottom of the pan. Also, baked potatoes—fat, brown, oval lumps. She shut the door and lifted the lid of the saucepan on the stove. Green beans—raw, ready to cook. *Ugh.* She used to like them. But more and more, vegetables disgusted her. Still, she was willing to eat a bean to please her mother.

She turned on the faucet. Leaning against the sink as the water ran, she studied a patch of afternoon sun on the floor. It looked luscious, yellow and warm. A perfect spot to curl up in and—

Her mother thumped down the steps. She entered the kitchen, shutting the door behind her, phone still tucked against her ear. "Sweetie, turn off the water! It costs money, just like everything else around here." She hurried to the stove, starting the flame under the beans.

N. shut off the faucet, then turned it on again and filled a glass. It tasted wonderful, loosening her thirst, splashing down through her throat, flooding each vein.

"But, Tam, it's been two years! Even if he's living with that woman, even if I have to accept that, I've still got two kids to support! I get no money from him, no *nothing*. I don't even know where he is! Why doesn't he at least contact the kids? Why doesn't he—"

N.'s mother looked up, startled, as if surprised to find her daughter standing there. "Excuse me," she said into the phone. Then, to N., "There's a Coke left in the refrigerator. You can have it if you want."

N. raised her glass of water.

"Well, then—is your homework done?"

N. smiled and took the hint, strolling out of the kitchen, feeling the little lick of heat against her ankle as she walked through the patch of sun.

"Give it to me now—*now!* I want it, give it now—*now!*" N. glanced up from her history text, watching the crowd of kids surge toward the stage with each *now!* The new "Bang!" video from Dram Skeetch was playing, on the *More Tits Video* afternoon replay. The lead singer—Johnny or Jimmy or Jerry somebody—grabbed his crotch as he screamed into the mic, and a girl in the crowd pulled off her top, her breasts obviously exposed but blurred. N. looked down at her book, at a picture of Franklin Delano Roosevelt. Increasingly, neither history nor TV made any sense to her—both populated by people who understood nothing.

The front door opened, and Emmet, tall and thin, stepped into the room, his cheeks flushed. Doug Bracken, their neighbor, followed him.

N. leaned back in surprise.

"Hi," Doug said shyly, blushing. At fifteen, a year younger than her brother, a year older than N., he was as short and blond as Emmet was tall and brown. He lived maybe two miles down the road, in a small house in front of a large patch of woods, with his father. He was a nuisance—but not quite as stupid as he seemed.

"Hello." N. flicked her eyes from him back to the TV screen.

Johnny or Jimmy or Jerry was leering directly into the camera. Then the camera backed off and caught the bass player humping his guitar as the crowd screamed louder.

"You like them?"

"Huh?" N. turned to Doug and frowned.

"Dram Skeetch. They're terrific. I mean, don't you think?"

N. blinked. Doug Bracken could blush more shades of red than a pile of bricks. "They're a waste," she said, muting the sound.

His face changed color—to an even deeper red. "Oh, well. I mean, yeah."

Emmet tossed his jacket on a chair. Like her, he didn't get cold easily. Unless, that is, he'd gone a long time without food. But she suspected he wasn't hungry. "I was messing around in the woods and ran into Doug. I invited him to supper." He held her eyes with his own for a moment, then looked away.

"Dad's going out to dinner with Fiona," offered Doug.

His mother had died a few years ago, from breast cancer.

Everybody on the long road they lived on—which spiraled from suburbs to country quicker than you'd think possible—knew the story. Mr. Bracken, who managed the last independent hardware store in the county—at the suburban end of the road—was avidly courting Fiona Tony, a hostess at the busy Pig Pie Diner, a quarter mile past the Bracken residence, at the country end of the road.

For her part, Fiona was avidly pretending she had six guys courting her, not just one. Everybody knew it was only a matter of time before she looked in the mirror and discovered she wasn't getting any younger, and decided that Mr. Bracken was a pretty good deal.

N.'s own father—The Man Who Went Away—used to manage and write for the *Frontier*, a local newspaper, producing, among other things, a popular general interest column called "Whimsey." Now he did— what? Who knew? He'd left a confusing note about needing to be with some woman—one he didn't bother to name—then disappeared.

N. pushed herself farther into the warmth of the cushions, longing to curl up into a ball and sleep. She knew exactly why Emmet had invited Doug over for dinner—to distract their mother and cover his lack of appetite. One less night of being fussed over, examined, pried at, spied upon—even though their mother, hapless as ever, never figured out anything.

Emmet disappeared into the kitchen. Doug hesitated a moment, then sat down on the other end of the couch. A commercial for 7-Up came on. N. clasped her hands and pushed her arms in front of her, then over her head, in a delicious stretch that ran all the way down her spine.

"So, are you doing that assignment thing about fathers?"

She laughed. "No. Are you?"

"Well, yeah. I mean, we're supposed to. Everybody is. Aren't we?" His pale blue eyes met hers, then danced away, as he commenced to turn another shade of red.

The superintendent of their school district had dreamed up what he called the Father Project. Every kid in the district was supposed to write an unsigned essay or poem or story about his or her father. Whether you loved him or not. Whether he lived with you or not. Whether he was married to your mother or not. Whether he was dead or alive or MIA. Whether he was widowed and courting a thirty-eight-year-old hostess at the Pig Pie Diner, or married and frolicking with his twenty-year-old girlfriend in a motel room. The anonymous results would be printed up in book form, with the intention of highlighting the importance of fathers to their children. Errant fathers were supposed to read it, feel bad, and mend their ways. Good fathers were supposed to read it, feel great, and continue being terrific.

It was rumored that the superintendent hoped his idea would go national. He'd already been written up in the *Frontier* and the larger *Mid-State News*, and several TV networks had contacted him.

A father, though, was of absolutely no importance to N. She had to concede, however, that somebody like Doug Bracken probably needed one.

Her mother, reading the letter of explanation about the Father Project that went home with every student, had scrunched up her face in distress. "Well," she'd said, trying to be reasonable. "Of course, fathers are important. I mean—" She'd looked over the letter at N. and Emmet. "I feel terrible that you don't have one anymore. I did my best, I did. I didn't leave *him*. He left *me*—"

At that her voice broke and she ran from the room. N. and Emmet let their eyes meet, then they both looked away. Their mother was the hardest part of their lives.

"—think they might get married."

"Huh?" What did he say? She needed to practice paying attention.

"Dad and Fiona. Maybe I should write an essay about that. Or maybe a poem. I could do a poem. Maybe something epic, like Lancelot and Guinevere. I could even work in King Author and Merlin. Except I keep thinking about my mother. Do you think she'll feel bad if Dad marries Fiona?"

She's dead, N. thought. *Why would she care?* "Probably not. Probably she just wants your father to be happy." That's what everybody always says, right? She felt a tightness in her stomach. "I'm hungry."

"Oh. Want a Fruitie?" Doug pulled a used-looking sheet of pressed fruit out of his back pocket and handed it to her. "This one's peach."

She hesitated, then unrolled the plastic and tore off a small strip. "Thanks," she said, trying to bite into it with her teeth. It was like chewing hard rubber.

Emmet came back in, carrying the Coke and a glass. "We've only got one left. I'll split it with you."

"That's okay. Give it to—"

"No," N. said, over dried fruit stuck to her teeth. "You and Emmet can have it." She'd come to hate fizzy liquids.

Her mother waltzed out of the kitchen, carrying a glass of ice, pleased to have a guest. "Doug, it's great to see you! You're more than welcome to stay. I'm sorry we're down to one Coke, but I haven't been to the store in a couple of days. Emmet, where are your manners? You didn't bring Doug any ice."

She handed the glass she was carrying to Doug. "Thanks," he said, smiling.

Emmet poured half the Coke over the cubes, keeping the can for himself. He still liked Coke, but he didn't like ice. N. could understand: strange frozen things banging around in your mouth, hurting your teeth. N. caught Emmet's eye and they both smiled a bit. The one thing that held them together was their shared, private knowledge:

Their ability to transform.

From:	Douglas Bracken <dougman@minimen.com>
To:	Dr. Rita I. Milton <Milton@tellet.com>
Sent:	Friday, November 08—5:05 PM
Subject:	Pressing Concerns

Dr. Milton, hi.

Is there a psychiatric way for me to tell the press that nobody got attacked, even though I said they did? I mean, nobody got hurt! Not really. Mom always said I had a good imagination. It's not our fault that a weirdo writer decided to disappear.

Mr. Brenner from the <u>Mid-State News</u> called the house again today and left another message. (His name is not so different from mine: Brenner and Bracken. Do you think that means something?) Anyway, Dad told me not to talk to anyone except the police and you, but I'm kind of embarrassed about the whole thing. Could you tell me what would be a good thing to say if I called this guy back, maybe anonymously? Something calm and convincing. I've seen psychiatrists on TV, and that's the way they talk. (You never answered whether you think I'm crazy or not. When he interviewed me, Chief Wilkinson said he didn't think I was, so that's a pretty good reference. Maybe you could talk to him? Dad says I'm okay, too.)

I wish kids at school would quit calling me a porno dork-face, though. There wasn't any sex involved! I got knocked out, I panicked and called the cops. Okay, somewhere along the line everybody's clothes fell off, but that's not exactly a federal crime. Is it? I hope you don't work for the FBI. (You don't, do you?)

Chief Wilkinson finally answered my e-mail. Did I tell you that? I really think that adults should be polite to kids and answer their mail promptly. Uv been great, by the way. (Ha! <u>Slumper!</u>)

Will Emmet be able to come home soon? I'm thinking about writing a poem about psychiatry. If I do, maybe you'd like to read it when it's done?

Gotta run. (My turn to cook!)

Doug Bracken
"Fear never met a greater foe,
 Than Dr. Freud and Dr. Milton,
 Talking to and fro."

I just made that up. Like it?

Emmet Marcona
Tomington Center—Wing A—Dr. Milton
Assignment
November 8

Niki's story is incredible! Even just the one section you've given me. Are you sure she wrote it? I mean, it's hers, there's no question that it's hers, she's always written stories and stuff, it's just—well, maybe I didn't realize how good she was.

You want to know if it's true? How can you even ask? It's a fantasy, which means <u>not true.</u> It's like Niki, though, to feed it to you a chapter at a time. That's the way it's always been between the two of us. She teases, offering a little bit of something, then maybe a little bit more. That's how she works.

But some of her story is true. Like the dinner with Doug. That happened. See, Doug likes Niki. That's why I invited him over for dinner that night. Niki got the fact of it right in her story, but not the reason.

I thought it would be good if she had a boyfriend, but she just didn't get it—that Doug liked her, I mean—even though we all rode the bus together to school every day, and he practically drooled all over her arm. I thought a boyfriend, a real one, might get her out of her head, out of her fantasies. See, underneath the surface, Doug's as solid as a stone. He's just the kind of person Niki needs.

You're right, Niki's a good actress—she can make-believe her way out of anything, and always could. It's her way of transforming experience into art—and yes, she'd probably be good on a stage. And you're also right that I'm not an actor at all. At least, not a good one. I admit, sometimes I'd like to be someone other than who I am. But how? You can't change what you are.

As for friends, I guess Doug's pretty much it. I'm not someone who's close to a lot of people. I used to be, at least somewhat, but frankly, I don't see the need anymore. I've come to know my own nature—which maybe not every sixteen-year-old kid can say, but I can. I'm a loner. I like being alone.

I did have a girlfriend, once. Steffi. But she happened, what, two years ago? I can't quite remember. She was pretty, with long, dark hair and green eyes. She liked me and I liked her, we held hands and kissed and stuff, but you couldn't compare us to other kids, or what you see in the movies and on TV—we didn't <u>do it</u>. But maybe you think that's strange.

What do I like to do? What I've already said, be by myself—walking in the woods, looking up through the trees at the sky.

See, the sky is like infinity or something, an endless

becoming. Nothing yet shaped, or rather, nothing yet finished or completed. Everything still a possibility. Birds are lucky, really. The sky is theirs. They get to be right in it.

These are just my thoughts. I'm writing them down so you'll let me go home.

Is "The Father Project" my own work? That's a really slimy thing to ask, Dr. Milton. Of course it is! I've been writing forever.

You think I stole it? And just who would I steal it from? I think you're trying to steal it from me!

Gosh golly gee, what are psychiatrists coming to these days?

I really don't have to cooperate with you at all. I'm only giving you my story so you'll know the truth and let Emmet come home. I hope you're not trying to medicate him out of his "condition." You can't change nature. You just can't.

Also—I'm a good writer, don't you think?

Meow!

P.S. I see you sent the same messenger. You might try prescribing a few pills for him. He could use them. I think he's depressed or something. Maybe he needs a girlfriend. It's gotta be tough to be so ugly and alone. Anyway, since he keeps staring at me, I'm writing this ONCE AGAIN with my back turned.

Slanger's World Is Narrow

By CARL BRENNER
Mid-State News staff writer

GANTON—Nicholas Slanger, the renowned author who's been missing for several days, apparently seldom left the run-down Gothic mansion he purchased three years ago outside of Ganton in Melville Co.

The "Munster Mansion," as it's called by locals, is situated at the end of a narrow, winding gravel drive, deep inside a large and formidable tract of woods. The house and surrounding forest emit an air of inhospitality.

According to locals at the Pig Pie Diner, a cheery restaurant at the edge of the same woods, Slanger kept to himself, but did occasionally come into the diner for takeout.

Janine Hawthorne, 47, who eats at the Pig Pie two or three times a week, said she's seen him exactly twice, and both times, "He wasn't nice at all." This sentiment was reflected by many others.

However, another diner, Carol Bruce, 26, said she ran into Mr. Slanger one night on her way to the Pig Pie during a rain shower, and he was, "absolutely charming, even a little flirtatious." Bruce continued, "All this stuff about him being mean just isn't true."

His publisher, Four Horses Press, released a bulletin expressing hope that Mr. Slanger will soon reappear. "We are concerned for his well-being, of course, but are confident of his safe return, as he has gone on 'sabbaticals' before. In fact, one time he remained completely out of contact for six months, only to turn up in France, where he was researching his next book, *Were-hearts*. Nicholas Slanger lives life on his own terms."

The 15-year-old boy who first reported the Halloween-night incident works at the Pig Pie as a dishwasher. Widely liked by the staff and other locals, he's been described by his boss, Russ Fink, as a "good kid, who got mixed up with some bad kids. This whole thing was just a big prank."

All three teens involved in the incident live near the woods. Mr. Slanger has no known close relatives.

THE FATHER PROJECT

Chapter Two

The girl made sure a green bean was speared on her fork, traveling to her mouth, every time her mother looked at her across the table. Sometimes she ate it; sometimes—if her mother turned back to Doug, speculating with him about the prospect of a match between his father and Fiona—she set it back on the plate.

The meatloaf was edible, even if the meat wasn't rare, as she more and more preferred it. But nobody made rare meatloaf. As for the baked potato—a potato was a potato, but loaded with butter it became its own little divinity.

"Well," said Doug, his slice of meatloaf slathered with ketchup, "on Monday, Fiona said *maybe* she'd go dancing with him this Saturday. You know, country style. She'd already agreed to go to dinner tonight, so that's like two dates in one week."

It was hard to imagine Mr. Bracken, with his round belly, going out dancing *any* style. N. watched Doug stick a hunk of potato in his mouth and keep talking.

"Dad bought a blue Western shirt and one of those string necktie things. It looks pretty good on him."

Doug was the only boy N. knew who spent time thinking about dances and weddings. But if you had a lonely father to marry off, maybe it became an occupational hazard. She blinked at her mother. Should she and Emmet try to marry *her* off?

"Fiona is a fool if she doesn't go with him," said her mother. "Oh, dear. I'm afraid this meatloaf is undersalted."

"No, it tastes great!" Doug exclaimed. "It sure beats a can of SpaghettiOs." He grinned at Emmet. "I'll have to run into you more often. What were you doing out in the woods, anyway?"

Emmet stopped pushing food around on his plate long enough to give Doug a piercing glare—one he quickly softened. "Oh, you know. Just messing around. I like being outdoors."

"He's gone all the time, now," N.'s mother complained to Doug. "Roaming around, hiking—always by himself. And he never dresses warmly enough."

"Yeah," said Doug. "Dad's always after me to wear more stuff." He stabbed a hunk of meatloaf, then glanced at N. "What about you? You like being outdoors, too?" He seemed to have a hard time focusing on her face, flushing a pale shade of pink and addressing his question to his plate.

N. pushed her red-gold hair behind her ears. Outdoors? Yes, she loved it. Yet, she was also drawn to the plush cushions on the living-room couch, especially in those increasingly rare moments when her mother, exhausted from teaching rowdy fifth graders all day, had the leisure to sit beside her, reading or watching television, idly stroking her arm or her hand or—if N. leaned and slumped against her—her head. She could spend hours on the couch, all but purring, basking in the heat of her own body, eyes shut, thinking of nothing much at all. That was a big difference between her and Emmet. She luxuriated in comfort, while he—

"Honey! Doug asked you a question."

"Yes," she answered automatically, noticing Doug's slightly stricken look. "I like it. I like the woods, too."

She glanced at Emmet; he looked away.

"Really?" Doug's face lit up. "If you want to come over sometime, there's this neat place I found in the woods back behind my house. It's like somebody cleared it out or something. There's even a log to sit on. If you wait quietly, sometimes animals come by. I've seen a fox several times, and deer—"

"Deer?" N.'s mother frowned. "Deer mean hunters, and this time of year—"

"Oh, it's safe. It's been posted *No Hunting* ever since Mr. Slanger moved into the Munster Mansion. He owns most of the woods now."

"Yes," N.'s mother said. "So I've heard." She reached for the butter dish. "Have you ever met him?"

Doug nodded. "Sort of. He came into the Pig Pie to pick up a roast beef sandwich." Doug worked at the diner on Saturdays, washing dishes. "I was really mad that I didn't have my copy of *Bloodwolf* with me, but he acted like he didn't want anyone to bother him, anyway." He wiped ketchup off his chin with his napkin. "I guess that's what happens when you become famous."

"I've heard he's not so bad, but maybe just shy. Lots of artists are introverts." Mrs. Marcona passed the butter dish to Emmet, who set it down. "But you're right, I don't think anyone would dare hunt on his land."

N. played with the food on her plate. She believed in the legend, debated back and forth at the Pig Pie, that Indians had lived here long ago, and knew the woods to be a place of magic—both good and bad. Animals changed into people. People changed into animals. Something stirred there.

She laughed silently, mashing the remaining potato on her plate into a pancake. Despite his books, Mr. Slanger didn't have the last say on what was real and what wasn't. Writing a story didn't change the truth.

"Eat your vegetables, sweetie!" Her mother frowned at her across the table, and N. obediently forked another bean.

Doug folded his last bite of meatloaf into a piece of bread. "You've seen the Munster Mansion, haven't you, Em?"

N. watched her mother pass Doug the plate of meatloaf.

"Thanks, Mrs. Marcona. I'd love some more." Doug slid a slice onto his plate and reached for the ketchup.

Emmet looked at N. as if from a far distance. "Yes, I've seen Slanger's house." His eyes went blank, and N. knew from just what angle he had seen it. A steep angle, looking down.

Her jaw clenched with the anger she could never quite escape.

Emmet was virtually without limit in what he could do. No height was too great. No distance too far. With his keen vision, harsh strength, and cold heart, he was powerful, ferocious, and free, while she—

She was confined to the ground, or, at most, to the top of a tree—a tree in which she was then trapped, too frightened to climb down. How many times, in the early days of their transformation—it must be two years ago now—had Emmet laughed at her clumsy attempts to mount the sky, climbing a tree trunk higher and higher, trying to match his upward soar.

How many times, early on, had he changed back into his boy's body and climbed after her, throwing her over his shoulder and hauling her—humiliated and hissing, ears pressed back, tail twitching—back down?

She'd finally come to understand a cold truth: she was earth, he was sky.

She hated him for that. He owned the air, but she could tread her way only through the woods—a minor creature among many. Why couldn't she be as powerful as he? One day, she might even be his prey.

If she could fight and defeat him, now, she would! And yet . . . N. swallowed hard, trying to calm herself. Emmet was her brother, and she his sister. Nothing could break that bond. They both hunted, craving the taste of blood, but never did they hunt each other.

That was their sacred rule.

"You are absolutely not going to walk home in the dark! I won't hear of it. That road is dangerous. No lights and no sidewalk."

N.'s mother went to hunt for her car keys, as Doug stood awkwardly by the door, ready to leave. Emmet picked up his jacket unhappily, anxiety tightening his mouth. He hadn't thought his invitation through—coming meant going, and going meant being out at night. Emmet hated the dark. It was filled with danger. Night was his time to withdraw, fold up, be safe—sleep.

N. loved the dark. "I'll ride along," she offered as her mother strode back into the living room. "Emmet has to study for a test." His face relaxed with relief, his harsh eyes communicating a thank-you. She smiled back. Now he owed her.

She caught Doug's suddenly brightened face. Why did he like her? He knew nothing.

"Get your jacket, then," her mother said, pulling on her own. "It's chilly out."

Emmet reached into the closet and tossed out her coat, and N. followed her mother and Doug into the night. The dark, beautiful night.

"Oh, look at that! Shoo! Another cat." Her mother stopped on the walk. "That's the second one I've seen around here. Strays, I guess." She turned toward N. "Have you noticed them? That one was black, but I keep seeing another cat. Older than a kitten, but not fully grown—a junior, I guess. Light orange."

N. froze. *Her mother had seen her?*

"I like cats," Doug offered cheerfully, as they resumed their walk to the car. "We used to have a gray tabby—Whiskers—but he got old and sick so we had to put him to sleep." He smiled at N., just as her mother unlocked the front car door and let out a wash of light, haloing his pale face. "Everybody thinks cats are aloof or something, but once you take the time to get to know them, they're really friendly. Sometimes I think they're supernatural or something, like they know more than we do."

N. blinked at him. He thought that? *Doug Bracken* thought that? What else did he know? She scooted into the backseat after him, staring at him through the dark. He stared back.

They headed for Doug's place—the last stop for the school bus the three of them rode every day. N. leaned back and studied the passing darkness, interrupted only by the occasional approaching headlight.

"So, Doug," her mother said, over her shoulder, a slight catch in her voice. "What do you think about that father thing? The assignment, I mean, about fathers."

Doug took his eyes off N., focusing on her mother. "I think it's terrific. I'm doing something about Dad and Fiona. Maybe a poem. I can do a poem." He glanced back at N.

"I see," said N.'s mother. "Well, you know, it's supposed to be anonymous. I mean, nobody's supposed to know real names or anything."

Doug shrugged in the darkness. "Everyone who lives around here goes to the Pig Pie Diner, and they all know about Fiona and Dad. The manager even has a wedding pool going, on when Dad's going to pop the question, and how long it takes her to say yes. Since I'm related to Dad, I'm not allowed to play."

N.'s mother laughed, then lapsed into silence. A couple more headlights passed them, then a car zoomed up from behind and cut around—no doubt trying to make it to the Pig Pie in time for the last piece of home-fried chicken. Another quarter mile and they'd be at Doug's.

"Well," her mother continued. "It's just that Mr. Marcona has been gone a couple of years now. What will my babies write about?"

Babies. N. hissed in disgust.

"Oh," Doug said, "I'm sure they'll think of something, especially now that he's back in the area."

N.'s mother slammed on the brakes, sending the car screeching off the road, zig-zagging and almost plunging into a ditch, before coming to a shuddering stop.

"Their father's back?" she whispered, clutching the steering wheel, staring out the windshield into the darkness.

The skin running up the back of N.'s neck grew tight—fur standing on end. She clenched her jaw against the teeth that elongated and sharpened in her mouth. She pushed her rear end hard into the seat, refusing the tail that pushed itself outward from her spine. She clutched her hands into fists, forbidding the claws that sprang from her nails.

Using all her strength, she stopped the cry in the back of her throat.

"Are you all right?" Doug touched her hand tentatively with his—a light, anxious stroke, a soft pat—and a yowl exploded from her lips.

"Honey, please," her mother said, voice shaking. "I know you're upset, but there's no need for that kind of language." Her voice broke altogether. "I can't believe he hasn't even called."

"I'm sorry, Mrs. Marcona. I'm really sorry. I thought you knew." Doug's eyes, shining in the dark, pleaded for forgiveness. "Dad saw him walking through the Pig Pie parking lot last Sunday night. We thought—"

"Of course you did," said N.'s mother, struggling for control. "You've done nothing wrong."

Rage exploded in N.'s head. O to fling herself into the night, race across the cold, black ground, and throw herself against prey—any prey! Slash, tear, kill. Snap bones, blood speckling her jaw.

Her mother started up the car, driving the short distance to Doug's house. N. felt a weight on her arm—Doug's hand, clutching her, as if trying to will her back.

"I'm sorry," he whispered.

Her anger collapsed as an image of her father flooded her heart. His dark, almost black hair, his quiet smile, his wide hands. "Hands for farming, not for writing," he'd sometimes say, laughing. "If a farmer can grow corn, I guess I can grow words." He'd wink at her, a beguiling mischief in his blue eyes.

He used to tickle her to make her laugh. He used to tuck her in at night.

He used to be hers.

The car stopped in front of Doug's, the porch light on. N. blinked as he opened the door. "Why," she asked, trying to breathe evenly, "was he at the Pig Pie?"

Doug stopped. "I don't know. Dad said hi to him, but he didn't answer. Fiona said he didn't come into the diner. Maybe he was going to use the phone." The Pig Pie had a phone booth next to the parking lot. "Dad said he looked upset and distracted, like he had something important to do and was worried he was too late." He glanced at her. "Dad's always late for stuff, himself."

"Well," said N.'s mother, her voice weak. "Whatever Mr. Marcona was concerned about, it obviously didn't have anything to do with us." She cleared her throat, dismissing Doug. "I'll wait till you're inside. Be sure to lock the door behind you."

"Okay, Mrs. Marcona. Thanks for the ride. And for dinner." He hesitated just a moment, then slid out.

On the way back home, N. cracked the window, letting the cold air bathe her face. She absorbed the passing darkness, her eyes wide, her mind blank. She could sit that way for hours, seeing nothing—until something, the smallest movement, the tiniest motion, caught her attention, snapping her body rigid.

Tonight, though, she saw nothing.

N. went upstairs and tapped on Emmet's door, finding him already in bed, sheltered beneath his quilt against the darkened room. He only blinked when she told him that Mr. Bracken had seen their father. As she turned to leave, he mumbled just four words: "Doesn't matter, does it?"

She shuddered violently. Yes, it did matter! He was their father! She gasped, squeezing her eyes shut, clenching her hands into fists. *And he'd left her behind.*

"Are you okay?" Emmet asked, his voice now bright with worry.

She looked at her brother, wrapped tightly in his blanket. He was so easily frightened. He needed her to be okay. "Yes," she said, willing her muscles to relax. "I'm fine."

And she was. Her father be damned. She had Emmet. Emmet had her.

Emmet Marcona
Tomington Center—Wing A—Dr. Milton
Assignment
November 9

How can Niki know so much about me? Reading her story—I mean, she's making everything up, but—

It's true what she says about my quilt, though, about me lying under it. I do that a lot. It makes me feel safe. There's nothing wrong with feeling safe, is there?

I admit I'm afraid of the dark. The aides come in and check me on their rounds every night, waving a flashlight in my face, but it doesn't help—it almost makes it worse. I know they don't like me. This one guy glares the light right in my eyes, like he's studying me. I bet Niki would say he looks like a weasel. He does, a little. She'd also tell him to go to hell. Me, I just lie there, paralyzed.

I don't know how Niki found out about my fear, but obviously she did. It started—I don't know when. Long before I came here. In the daytime, all I want is to be out, walking or staring at the sky. But at night, something comes over me. It's fear, plain and simple. I curl up and hide under my quilt. It's not something I want a lot of people to know about.

But who would find out, anyway? Doug's the only one who still wants to be friends with me. People make fun of him sometimes, but they underestimate him. Maybe our friendship is over now, though. He hasn't come to see me.

Not that anybody else has. Why won't you let Niki visit? And Mom came only the one time. I know it's a long drive, and she's got her hands full right now, taking care of Niki. She can't be everywhere.

Still, I wish she hadn't looked at me so strangely when she was here, as if she didn't know who I was. We've never been close—but still, I'm her son.

She's probably just under a lot of stress, and that's why she's stayed away. She'd probably get even more upset if she knew I was afraid of the dark.

I wonder if Mom blames me for making Dad go away. He always charmed the ladies—Mom, Niki, half the women he met. "Charismatic" is the word people used about him. People wondered why he hadn't gone further in his career. I don't have an answer for that. All I know is that in contrast to him, I was a dud. I mean, I saw how he acted around Niki. Like she was the sun in his day, the moon in his night.

Me, I was a big disappointment. Whenever we argued, I ran and hid in my room.

Except for one time. But maybe I wish I had run away then, too.

To outsiders, our family probably looked okay. And

maybe we were. Mom had her fifth graders and a husband everyone liked. Dad had Niki—they were always close, always happy to be together, always a good match. I was—there. So we were all connected somehow.

Then everything fell apart. In a way, I wasn't surprised to find out Dad was having an affair—he always liked to flirt. Still, it was a shock. I could see him leaving Mom and me—we're the dull ones in the family. But Niki? Maybe Dad was one of those men who simply have to move on, no matter what kind of mess they leave behind.

When I'd listen to Mom go on about Dad, about losing him, I just wanted to say, "Hey, that's what men do. They leave. Don't take it so personally." But she might have figured out that I wanted to leave.

To be honest, I don't really know what's going on with Mom. Inside, I mean. I think she planned to be more than a wife and a mother and a fifth-grade teacher. Did she tell you that she won some major short-story contest in college, that she wanted to write novels? Instead, she married Dad—she couldn't resist him, she'd say—a journalist, who ended up managing a small newspaper and writing a personal interest column. Maybe she felt trapped and wanted to leave, but Dad beat her to it.

See, family has a way of holding you down, even

when you want to fly away. Sometimes I think I can feel the sky pulling me, urging me upward. As if I could really fly. That's crazy, I know. Niki stuff. But it's a common-enough wish, isn't it, to want to fly?

I sometimes wonder if that's what happened to Dad. That there wasn't another woman, and never was. That he just felt the sky pulling him, and he flew away.

That night of the dinner with Doug, Niki came into my room when they got back from taking him home—just like she said in her story—and told me Dad had been seen in the area. It surprised me, but I stayed calm.

I knew Niki wanted it to be true, but I suspected that Doug's father had seen someone who just looked like Dad. He's never coming back.

Look, Dr. Milton, I'm writing all of this down for you, when I really don't want to—it's really none of your business—so can you give me something back?

I've only got a thin cotton blanket here. At night, I wrap myself up in it as tightly as I can, but it's not enough. Could you get me a thicker blanket, maybe even a quilt?

The night still scares me.

From: Douglas Bracken <dougman@minimen.com>
To: Dr. Rita I. Milton <Milton@tellet.com>
Sent: Saturday, November 09—5:11 PM
Subject: Re: Friendship with Niki and Emmet Marcona

Dear Dr. Milton,

I'm glad you liked my little poem! It was just a snippet, really. I can do more! You're right--English is my favorite subject. My father thinks it's good that I apply myself to the study of words. He's into hardware, himself.

You don't think Niki wrote her own story? Who else could have written it? I doubt Mr. Slanger did! (I mean, if he wasn't missing. Pretty cool if he did, though, huh? You could get his autograph!) I'm sure if Niki gave it to you, it's hers. She doesn't mess around. And two years ago she won first prize in the school essay contest, so for sure she's good. I think writers like to hide a lot behind their words.

I've known her and Emmet since we moved here--about four years, I guess. Not that we're always together. To be honest, Niki and Emmet seemed OK to just hang with each other. I thought sisters and brothers fought all the time, but not them. Niki always stands up for Emmet, because he's kind of sensitive. And he's always trying to keep her from getting into trouble--she's got a temper! Anyway, we live a couple of miles from each other, and there's no sidewalk or anything, so that makes it a little hard to get together. It's kind of rural out here, to tell you the truth--except we're close to the Pig Pie Diner.

Have you ever eaten there? Try their Southern Fried Steak sometime. It's great! And you get these really big French fries with it. A strawberry shake completes the meal! That's what Fiona says about a shake. She has a real understanding of food, and the need to eat it. Did I mention that she's engaged to my Dad? Except they keep changing the wedding date, so keep your fingers crossed. I'm worried that she's nervous now because of all the stuff that happened in the woods. Except nothing major happened! I really wish I'd never called the police. And Carl Brenner is a jerk, don't you think? Niki and Emmet are <u>not</u> bad kids! Except he's right that everybody at the Pig Pie likes me.

Anyway, if you ever want to meet me in person, we could get together at the Pig Pie. (In case you're wondering what I look like, I'm short, but have blond hair, so I think that helps make up for a lot of things. Nobody's called me handsome yet, but it could happen.) (Also, I could wear a name tag, if that would help.) I work at the diner on Saturdays, washing dishes, and get my lunch free, so you would only have to pay for your own meal.

You want to know about my mom? She died three years and two months ago, from breast cancer. She already had it before we moved here, but we thought she was OK. Then--it all came back, worse. It's hard to think about. Anyway, that's why Dad's getting married again. Or trying to. I think Mom's death made me a little bit psychic or something. I'm kind of tuned into Niki and Emmet because their father left them. I mean, I know what it's like to only have one parent, although my mother never did anything disgusting like run off with someone else. Mrs. Marcona is really nice, and I always thought Mr. Marcona was OK, if a little, um--Dad would say he was <u>satisfied</u> with himself--so I don't know what happened. I don't see how it could have had anything to do with the woods or Mr. Slanger, though.

Dr. Milton, I can assure you that Emmet would never hurt anyone. As for Mr. Marcona, he might have left for Europe or something. I think men do that a lot, when they have mistresses.

I have to stop now, so I can start dinner. We're having baked chicken. I dunk it in milk and eggs beaten together, then dip it in crunched-up cornflakes. Have you ever tried it that way? It's not bad. Plus we're having Tater Tots and frozen asparagus (cooked).

Best wishes, and hoping to hear from you,
Doug Bracken
"Cornflaking, chicken baking,
 Even shrinks
 Got hungry-making,
 Freud-related thoughts."

Pretty good, huh?

I'm sorry, too, Dr. Milton, that my computer is too old and dumb to e-mail my story to you. Crash and burn, crash and burn. Until Mom gets around to buying me a new one, we'll just have to rely on hand delivery.

Boo-hoo!

And, ONCE MORE, of course it's my work. Haven't you ever heard of child geniuses? Don't give me that stuff about my mother wanting to be a writer. So she won a prize once in college. Big whoop. As she's already told you, she gave up that notion a long time ago—and gladly—when she had us. Now she writes out class plans every night for her fifth graders—whom she's CRAZY about, in case you haven't noticed—and is your basic happy mother. Or will be, when Emmet comes home and she can go back to work.

Now, about weasel-face. Has he got the hots for you? He seems suspiciously loyal to such a run-and-fetch-it job. A boy toy for the doc? Yuck. Warning: he's already a cheat! If you want me to keep giving him my story, tell him to stop looking at me that way—you know. My dad would have cheerfully ripped his, um, face off. He was like that.

Who Else Is Missing?

by CARL BRENNER
Mid-State News staff writer

GANTON—Nicholas Slanger is not the only man who's gone missing from the Ganton area.

The father of the two teenagers who purportedly attacked Mr. Slanger on Halloween night apparently left his wife and children two years ago to live with another woman. Surprisingly, no one in the area seems to know her identity. Nothing has been heard from the man since.

According to Chief Wilkinson, there is no reason to tie his "disappearance" to that of Slanger's. "Sadly, some men abandon their families, and don't necessarily leave a forwarding address," Wilkinson said, in reply to a reporter's questions. "However, we would like to talk to him, and are trying to determine his location."

The teenagers' mother has refused to speak with the press. Local residents want to know if they need to be worried about a serial killer. According to Miller Brooks, who dropped by the Pig Pie for a cup of coffee and a doughnut, "We're all a little nervous. Nicholas Slanger never made himself a part of the community, but he's a famous person who's missing, and of course we wonder why. We're hoping he's not dead. And ditto about [the father of those kids]."

Chief Wilkinson says the investigation is continuing.

THE FATHER PROJECT

Chapter Three

The girl waited for the bus with her brother. Backpack slung over his shoulder, Emmet stood silently, occupied with studying the blue morning sky, a look of longing on his face. N. resisted the urge to bump against his leg to remind him of her presence. He hated touch—he found it unbearable, and her habit of needing it, incomprehensible.

Leaving him alone, she watched a red leaf tumbling from a maple tree, torn between wanting to run and grab it, and simply wanting to watch it tumble. The yellow school bus had barreled past a while ago, empty of students, on its run to the parking lot at the Pig Pie Diner, where it would turn around and head back to pick up its first customer—Doug Bracken.

The red leaf landed gracefully on the ground, and the girl's muscles bunched—she wanted to pounce. But a roar distracted her and she turned to face the road as the yellow bus bore down on them, screeching to a thunderous halt. She climbed in ahead of Emmet, signaling for him to follow—he dreaded being confined, and always held back. She waved to Doug Bracken.

"Hey, guys," he called to them, getting up from the back of the bus to move forward, smiling uncertainly, his face painted with an anxious hope.

"Hey," said N. She poked Emmet—he flinched, then lifted his hand. "Hey, Doug," he said.

Doug took the seat behind them. N. and her brother had long ago broken the ancient rule of ignoring your sibling. Emmet could no longer bear sitting next to anyone, and used N. as a shield. N. increasingly had trouble resisting leaning against whoever was beside her, boy or girl, hoping they'd reach out and absentmindedly scratch her head. She'd almost gotten kicked on the floor by Debba Watson, who had a large, inviting lap. And when Buck Fallow had grinned and squeezed her thigh, she'd slashed at him, leaving a thin, bright scratch across his cheek. Emmet had had to do the unbearable—*be a brother*—grabbing N.'s arm and yanking her back to his seat, threatening Buck with a killer's cold stare.

After that, they sat together—not that anyone, except Doug, wanted to have anything to do with them anymore. N. tried not to lean against Emmet. Emmet tried not to shriek out loud when she forgot and did.

"So, how you guys doing?" asked Doug, his eyes bright with uncertainty.

N. half turned to face him as the bus screeched to a stop in front of the first truly suburban house on the road, picking up Samantha Kaylo and Debba Watson and Chas Bowen. The bus jerked forward again.

"We're okay," she answered. "You?"

"Um, yeah. I really liked your mom's meatloaf last night."

She shrugged. "It's better rare."

"Oh. Really?" Doug looked puzzled. Since he'd started working Saturdays at the Pig Pie, he'd managed to sample everything on the menu. N. could almost see him clicking through the list of entrées, trying to find a rare meatloaf. "I like my food well done."

"Most people do."

Doug nodded toward the back of Emmet's head. "Is he okay? I mean, about, um"—he lowered his voice—"your father? The way he showed up, but didn't show up?"

"Yes." N. nudged Emmet and he slowly turned his head, then his neck, then his upper body to face Doug, almost banging knees with N. She quickly scooched away so they didn't touch.

"I'm fine," he said quietly but firmly. He looked at Doug and N. as if he sat on a high, imposing branch of a tree, then turned back.

"Um, I've got something to give you. You'll never believe who—" Doug began, but N. smiled and turned around as well, effectively ending their conversation. He talked too much. She closed her eyes.

When she blinked them open again, the bus was full of noisy kids. As they pulled into the Wexford High parking lot, she realized the tension pressed against her face was Emmet—she'd fallen asleep against his arm. He looked at her, mouth tight, arm trembling, eyes caged and wild.

She sat up. Poor Emmet. One more touch and he'd scream. She had no way to comfort him. She smiled and he relaxed slightly. Waiting until almost everyone had cleared the bus, they filed off.

"I've got something for you," Doug began again, grabbing Emmet's arm, hurriedly letting go when he jerked back, squawking, mouth open.

"It's okay," said N., prodding Emmet toward the front door of the school. "He just didn't get much sleep last night."

"But—"

"See you," she said, moving forward. It was getting difficult to deal with regular people.

Skipping her fourth-period class, N. practiced hiding in the open. She stood still, body compressed—clutching her math book, not moving a muscle—just down the hall from the administrative offices. Beside her stood a free-standing, A-frame display board plastered with notices about band practice and the debate club. Neither Mr. Dunbar, the assistant principal, nor Mrs. Nanglit, the school secretary, noticed her as they stood outside the offices, talking. N. had chosen well, hiding just at the edge of their peripheral vision.

Mr. Dunbar rifled through a batch of papers in his arms. "Here's the transfer information on that new student, Springler David. Springler David? That can't be right. Oh, David Springler. They wrote it backwards." He chuckled as he handed the folder to Mrs. Nanglit, his eyes traveling right past N.

She didn't respond—the slightest movement would ruin both her technique and her cover. The point was to remain so still that you were obviously invisible, while obviously present. That's how prey was tricked, and won.

"And about that incident with the Marcona kid—darn." The pile of papers spilled from his arms, and both he and Mrs. Nanglit bent to retrieve them.

Marcona kid? Incident? N. froze, shrinking her body even smaller, forcing her heart to pound itself senseless in her chest without any accompanying body movement—one twitch and she'd be noticed.

Mr. Dunbar and Mrs. Nanglit resurfaced at the same time, exchanging and rearranging papers.

"The Marcona kid?" asked Mrs. Nanglit. "Which one?"

"The boy, Emmet. Apparently Jeff Johnson was teasing him in gym, shoving up against him and stuff, and Emmet lost it. *Bit* the kid. Or tried to. Jeff said Emmet stabbed him in the arm with his mouth, which doesn't make any sense. Fortunately he didn't break any skin."

Mr. Dunbar shook his head. "Mrs. Marcona came to get him half an hour ago. Did you know she teaches over at Gunsdale Elementary? She had to leave her class and everything. Her son is definitely a therapy case." He found the sheet he was looking for and handed it to Mrs. Nanglit. "Those Marcona kids are strange."

Mrs. Nanglit nodded her head. "*Too* strange. The way that girl looks at you is creepy. Like she wants to eat you for supper."

"Well," Mr. Dunbar said as they headed into the office, "you know how it is. Broken family. No father at home. The usual. Maybe the Father Project will change things." He laughed. "Fat chance, right?" They disappeared inside.

N. slunk down on a seat by herself as the bus filled up with kids. She felt naked and exposed without Emmet. Kids stared at her as they strode down the aisle or turned in their seats—all of them whispering Emmet's name.

She trembled. He must have started to break form, jabbing that kid with his beak, pulling himself back at the last second. What if he'd actually transformed? She shuddered, closing her eyes. It was too horrible to think of. Would she and Emmet have to leave, find a way to live by themselves in the wild? How could they take care of each other?

Someone sat beside her. Her eyes shot open, nails sharpening.

Doug Bracken. Her nails retracted.

He held his head up defiantly, ignoring the hoots and jeers of the other kids.

"Hey, Doug," Buck Fallow called from the back of the bus, "better stay away from those Marconas. Her brother bit Jeff Johnson."

"Yeah," someone else chimed in. "What a loon. The way he went after Jeff, he looked just like a giant bird. Gawk! Gawk!"

A harsh chorus boomed through the bus as everyone squawked and clucked and chirruped. Frightened, N. peered over her shoulder just in time to see Buck Fallow flapping his arms and darting his head forward. "The human bird boy!" he cried. "At least being *animal* runs in the family. The brother's got a beak, and the sister's got claws. And I should know!" He guffawed. "You know what kind of girl *she* is—snatch 'n' scratch!"

N.'s face flamed red, and she slunk back down in her seat, rage and fear pounding in her chest. Doug stared straight ahead, his mouth tight, but he didn't move away.

"A beak!" a kid squealed in a shrill voice, pretending to be scared. "A beak!"

"Hiss!" someone yelled.

"That's it!" Buck bellowed. "Beak Boy and Hiss!"

"Quiet down, you guys!" yelled the driver. "Or this bus is not moving!"

The voices stopped—everyone wanted to go home.

As the bus started up, it was all N. could do to keep her shape. She had to forcibly restrain herself from scrambling over Doug's lap, tearing down the aisle, leaping into Buck Fallow's face, and clawing his eyes out. She trembled, exhausted from the effort.

It was only as the first group of kids was dropped off that she realized Doug was stroking the back of her hand, trying to calm her. She slumped against his arm, seeking comfort—then hurriedly pulled away.

She couldn't lean against Doug—he *liked* her! A low snarl sounded in her throat, and he quickly pulled his hand back—but she immediately felt sorry, already missing his warmth. He was only being kind.

"Don't pay any attention to them," he said, crooking his mouth in a weak attempt at a smile. "They're stupid jerks. They can't even tell when someone needs help."

Needs help? N.'s eyes narrowed. Doug thought that she and Emmet needed help? A quiet growl rumbled in her chest. How dare he! As if he knew anything. As if—

She stopped, noting that his shoulder was higher than hers. He must have been growing recently. She slouched back in the seat and closed her eyes, letting the bus conveniently rock her close to his arm again. Other than the hunt, heat and comfort were her deepest needs.

"This is your stop," Doug said, nudging her awake. She blinked her eyes open, then sat up. *Home.* Climbing off the bus, she stood across the street from her wood-frame house, the high attic windows glinting in the afternoon sun. Sensing something, she turned to find Doug standing behind her. He shrugged, watching the bus pull away, continuing its run to the Pig Pie parking lot, then he trailed her across the road.

"I'm sorry Em got sick," he said, his face pink, as they stood in her front yard. He reached into his backpack and pulled out a letter. "This is what I had for him." He hesitated, studying N. carefully, and for just a moment she thought he knew—

No, that was crazy. He knew nothing. He was just a boy with a bad case of loneliness, looking for a friend.

"While I was waiting for the bus this morning, that weirdo—Mr. Slanger—drove by my house and stopped. He handed me this envelope and said to give it to Emmet." He stared at it as if he didn't quite believe it was real, then looked at N. "He didn't even say hi! Just, *'Give this to Emmet Marcona.'* He didn't even offer me an autograph." Perplexed, N. took the envelope. "Mr. Slanger gave it to you?" The writer? Why would he be giving anything to Emmet?

The front door of the house opened, and N.'s mother stuck her head out. "Come inside, would you? I need your help!" Then, her voice flat, "Oh, hello, Doug." She didn't invite him in.

"Well," he said, "I'd better go." He smiled weakly. "Tomorrow night is the big country dance. Fiona said she'd go with Dad. Thirty-seven people have money down on when he pops the question." He waited a moment for a reply. Getting none, he shrugged, his face growing crimson, and turned to walk home, making his way down the edge of the road. There was plenty of light left in the afternoon, but still no sidewalks.

"Be careful," N. called after him, surprising herself. Now, why did she say that? He turned and waved, grinning. "Okay," he answered, walking backward until he almost tripped. He turned face-forward, continuing on his way.

N. fingered the stiff envelope, and went inside.

From: Douglas Bracken <dougman@minimen.com>
To: Dr. Rita I. Milton <Milton@tellet.com>
Sent: Sunday, November 10—11:02 AM
Subject: Reporters!

Dr. Milton,

This morning's <u>Sunday Start</u> on Channel 4 had this huge report on the investigation! Did you see it? Sadie Fuller practically said we were sicko teens, having sex in the woods at night or something, like it was Satanic. Really! Why are TV reporters such slimeballs? I used to think Sadie Fuller was <u>nice</u>.

We were just going for a walk. I <u>told</u> everybody that. Even though we ended up sort of naked, nobody did anything porno! Honest. It was just a clothing mishap, in the midst of chaos. And I just about froze my you-know-what off. The show made us sound like disgusting teen sluts. We were just, you know, kids in the woods.

Mr. Slanger wasn't there. It's not our fault he disappeared the same night. Nobody's dead!

The show practically said that the reason I changed my story was diabolical. But I told the police the truth--that I was spooked, I hit my head and my brain didn't work right until the next day. Chief Wilkinson understood completely. I mean, haven't you ever been spooked before? When I was little, I was scared to go downstairs to the basement. It was dark, and there were spiders. Once my mom asked me if I'd brought up the rake from the basement like she'd asked me to do, and I said I had, but I hadn't. <u>Spooked!</u> I hid in the bathroom for a while, until she gave up and went and got it herself. Don't you think that was a legitimate lie? (I <u>did</u> help her rake the yard later, and it's not like she didn't still love me and stuff.)

Dad's totally freaked out, and just chased off another TV truck. Do you have any advice for older men that I could pass on to him? We're staying inside today. Sort of hibernating.

Doug Bracken
"Too upset to rhyme"

Douglas Bracken <dougman@minimen.com>
To: Dr. Rita I. Milton <Milton@tellet.com>
Sent: Sunday, November 10—3:31 PM
Subject: Me Again

Dr. Milton,

Maybe I was too excited or something in my last e-mail? It's not like I'm crazy or anything. Did Emmet see the show? I don't know if he can watch TV where he is. I kind of hope he didn't see it, since he's so upset about everything. He's like a bird that keeps flying into glass windows. And the stuff about him and Niki being so weird--gosh, poor Em. I'm not really worried about Niki--she'd laugh it off. But her mother probably isn't too happy. Judging from Dad's reaction.

Dad thinks <u>Sunday Start</u> is bad TV. He's probably right, except Sadie Fuller is kind of hot, even though she's way too old for me. If Mr. Slanger had been there, like Sadie suggests, shouldn't <u>he</u> be the one accused of being porno? I mean, if he was, like, watching us or something? Except there wasn't anything to watch.

I'm confused.

So far, we've had 33 phone calls from nosy people and reporters. Dad told them all to go to hell. Maybe there's some psychiatric stress-relieving stuff he could do?

Doug Bracken
"Still too upset
 To place a bet
 On when this mess
 Will be forget."

(poetic license)

Emmet Marcona
Tomington Center—Wing A—Dr. Milton
Assignment
November 11

Thank you for the extra blanket. It helps.

And yes, I'm sure you're right—Mom would visit if she could. Would you tell her that I miss her?

Reading Niki's story, as strange as it is, helps me feel less alone. I wish I could talk to her about it.

It's not true that I bit someone. Jeff Johnson—the kid at school—yes, he was bugging me. Pushing me, actually. And I can't stand that, being shoved. So I pushed back, I had to, to get him off, but I stumbled and fell, crashing into his arm, face-first. Honest. But everybody started yelling, "Coach! Emmet bit Jeff! He bit him!" Crazy bunch of crap.

Okay, it scared me, I ran out of the room. I hate gym anyway. Hate being so close to all those kids. I shouldn't have to take gym at all. Or even be in school. I can't stand to be around people. Can't stand to be touched.

Niki knows. I don't how she knows so much about me, but she does. She's learned all my weaknesses. She leans against me when I can't push her away, like on the school bus, even though she knows I can't bear it. She falls asleep against my arm, and what am I supposed to do? It isn't natural to lean against a brother like that—or touch him. I think she only does it to psyche me out—it's a game with her. When she knows I'm totally freaked, she pulls back and grins like a Cheshire cat.

Who was it—Steffi, that girl I told you about. She touched me, we held hands. Touch was okay then. I liked it, I remember liking it. I think. But now—I'm just different.

I've been changing somehow. Ever since—well, I don't know. A year ago, two years? I guess I've just become more of who I am. A hermit, probably. One of those guys who ends up living by himself in the woods.

Like Mr. Slanger.

Mom got all hysterical when the school called. Now, why did they have to do that, call her and get her upset? She was just starting a new relationship—did she tell you about that? It was a secret—she didn't know I knew, but I overheard her on the phone, talking about it to Aunt Tam. I figured it was with someone she worked with at school. I didn't dare tell Niki, though.

Anyway, I suppose things were looking up for Mom—even if, for me, they were looking down. She didn't need new trouble in her life. I stumbled, that's all. Fell against a kid's arm with my face. I had to go lie down in the nurse's room afterward, but that was because I was rattled by all the noise and attention, not because I'd bitten someone.

There's nothing wrong with me. I'm not crazy. I didn't do anything to Jeff on purpose, not that day or any other day. The last thing I want to do is touch someone—much less bite them. I can't even imagine touching Niki anymore. And she's the one closest to me.

I like to be alone. Can't we leave it at that?

Milton and Weasel
Sitting in a tree,
K-I-S-S-I-N-G.
First comes love,
Then comes marriage,
Then comes Milton with a baby carriage.

No? So he's just your, like, go-boy or
something? What fun is that? You need to
get out more.
    So, what's on for today? More
psychotherapy for people who don't need it?
What fun is that? You need to get out more.
Oops! I'm repeating myself.

Psychiatrist Silent

by CARL BRENNER
Mid-State News staff writer

GANTON—*Mid-State News* has learned, from an unnamed source, that Nicholas Slanger was formerly a patient of Dr. Rita I. Milton, of the Tomington Center for Psychiatric Disorders.

Dr. Milton has refused all comment. The Tomington Center, which treats patients with serious mental disorders, issued the following statement: "We do not release information to the press." The Center is known to be treating one of the teenagers accused of attacking Mr. Slanger.

According to the source, Slanger, a man known for his secretive ways, apparently spent two months at Tomington three years ago. He then settled in his "Munster Mansion," outside of Ganton, in order to continue his treatment, as an outpatient, with Dr. Milton. It is not known how long his treatment continued.

Four Horses Press, his publisher, says, "We do not pry into Nicholas Slanger's private life. Success does not come without a price, and it is not unusual for those who have achieved the status Mr. Slanger has to seek help in dealing with stress. If true, it hardly speaks against his character."

Chief Wilkinson had no comment.

THE FATHER PROJECT

Chapter Four

The girl's mother, her eyes frantic, clutched her arm as soon as she stepped through the front door. "Did you hear? Emmet attacked a boy at school! He bit him! I had to go get him. I—" She stopped speaking, pressing her hands against her face.

"This is crazy," she continued, her face pale. "It doesn't make any sense." N. saw the fear in her eyes. "Thank God, that kid wasn't hurt. But why would Emmet do such a thing? He's never been in trouble before, never hurt *anyone*. It must be your father—and that Father Project thing. It's upsetting him. That has to be it."

She took N.'s arm, dragging her up the steps, pulling her toward Emmet's bedroom. N.'s muscles tensed. Who was her mother to drag *her*? She wasn't some *dog*. But when her mother stopped in front of Emmet's door, fear turning her eyes dark, N. submitted.

"He's lying down now," her mother explained. "He looks terrible. The earliest the doctor can see him is the end of next week. Of course, Emmet doesn't think he needs to go."

N. tried to picture Dr. Lee peering into Emmet's cold, distant eyes.

Her mother rattled on, staring at his door. "I gave him some aspirin—he said he had a headache—and told him to get some sleep. I left a message with Aunt Tam, so she should be calling soon. Oh, honey, I'm just so scared!"

N. dropped her backpack and jacket on the floor. How could she help Emmet if her mother's fear engulfed them all? "I'm sure he'll be fine," she said. "He just—"

"What's that?" her mother interrupted, eyeing the envelope still clutched in N.'s hand. "I already brought in the mail."

"Oh, just something Doug gave me," N. answered, folding it over and stuffing it into her pocket. "Nothing important."

The phone rang downstairs. "That must be Aunt Tam," her mother exclaimed, relief chasing the worry out of her face. She practically pushed N. into the closed door. "Talk to your brother, please. Find out what's wrong. He won't confide in me." She disappeared down the stairs.

N. waited a moment, then tapped. Getting no response, she opened the door. Emmet, buried under his quilt up to his chin, blinked awake, watching her silently, his face pale and unhappy. She crossed the room. Slipping off her shoes, she perched at the foot of his bed, forcing him to rearrange his feet so they didn't come in contact with her. His eyes suddenly filled with tears, and he turned his head toward the window.

That surprised her. Other than the triumph that came with a successful hunt, he rarely expressed emotion anymore. N. could sense his body trembling under the quilt, and fought an urge to rub against his leg, giving him warmth and comfort. But touch would bring no comfort to Emmet. If tears proved him still human, a touch would prove him not.

"I can't stand it anymore," he said quietly, taking in the late October sky, his voice weak. "I need to transform. Completely. Permanently." He turned to look at her. "That idiot Jeff Johnson—he *touched* me! Made fun of me! I wanted to destroy him. I started to change—I didn't care if anyone saw me or not. Then I remembered, and stopped."

N. studied his thin face. Like him, she, too, longed to transform. Didn't she slip out of her human skin every day—every day that she could? Didn't she hunt, loving the chase, the pounce and the strike, her teeth sinking into flesh, blood spurting in her mouth? But there were days she failed at the hunt—too many days. And too many days that Emmet failed, as well. They were both still learning. How many times did they head home—N. grumpy and hissing, Emmet chilled and weak and hungry—to consume their mother's food?

She ran her fingers over the edge of Emmet's quilt. It was strange.

They still needed to retreat into their human bodies to survive. She didn't know why they were living this protracted half life. Anyone else— she twitched her nose—well, there wasn't anyone else, not like them. She didn't know why they transformed when others didn't. It was just—what they did. What they were. Ever since—

She blinked, confused. Ever since what?

"I can't wait much longer," Emmet said, his eyes distant and hungry. "All I want is the sky."

"It's too soon," she replied, not really knowing if that was true. "We're not ready to change completely. We'd starve." That was it—a simple answer to a simple question. Her mind, though, raced on, bringing her a swift, sharp headache.

Why did they transform, when others didn't? In her animal shape, she never thought to ask—she just *was*. In her human shape—well, if, in the beginning, she *had* asked, she'd long ago stopped. Increasingly, thoughts like these were a struggle.

"In the wild, we'd be feeding on our own," Emmet responded, his voice hollow. "We'd have left our mother long ago."

"We're still part human," she said, staring at the stupid socks on her feet—black, decorated with orange Halloween pumpkins. Her mother had bought them for her. Why had she worn them? "People take forever to grow up." She'd read that in school—how human offspring, compared to other animals, take years to mature. Why should she and Emmet be any different? "If you changed over now," she said, "I mean, completely—" She stopped.

"What?"

"We wouldn't know each other anymore." Her heart sprang open— an empty box. Without Emmet, she was nothing, she had no companion in the world, no one to love. Her mother might be good for the occasional pat on the head—her father could go to hell!—but Emmet was everything to her.

If they totally transformed, they'd be cat and bird of prey, separated by their very natures, with no common speech or link—and no way to help each other. She waited, her muscles surprisingly tense, for his response. Did he even care?

He turned his face toward the window again. "We wouldn't need to know each other," he said, "because we wouldn't *need* each other."

She hissed, wanting to smack him, draw blood from his skin. "We would, too! Just like we do *now*."

"We need each other less and less," he said. "In time—"

"That's what you think!" she yowled, feeling her nails sharpen, her muscles bunch in anger. "We need each other a lot!" One swipe across his face and—

"I'm hungry," he said.

She blinked. As his eyes went feral, she felt her anger relent, her muscles begin to relax. "Okay," she finally said, sliding off the bed. "I'll be back in a minute."

She left his room, heading down the back steps to the kitchen. Her mother's voice rose and fell from the dining room. Good. She was still talking to Aunt Tam.

On the counter was a chuck roast her mother had taken out to finish defrosting. She poked it with her finger—it was almost thawed. Lucky! N. quickly undid the plastic wrap, and, getting out a knife, cut off several long, thin strips, her fingers growing sticky with blood. She wrapped the roast back up—it didn't look too violated—and put the slices on a plate. Making sure her mother was still talking, she slipped back up the steps to Emmet's room.

"Here," she said, sitting beside him on the bed. "Open up."

He pushed himself half upright against his pillow, and opened his mouth like a baby bird. She slid in a slice of raw meat, and when he had finished chewing and swallowing, another, then another. His color seemed to improve as he ate, his spirits rejuvenate.

"Thanks," he said at last, a small smile on his face. She watched his eyes blink shut, and waited beside him as he sank into the safety of his quilt, the comfort of sleep.

She licked the blood off her fingers.

*   *   *

"How's Emmet?" asked her mother, coming into the kitchen just as N. finished rinsing off the plate.

"Oh, he's fine," N. said, smiling. Maybe later, her mother would sit beside her in front of the TV, absentmindedly stroking her arm or head. "He just didn't have enough to eat today—that's why he snapped at that kid. I fixed him some food. He's asleep now."

"You mean he was just hungry?" asked her mother, astonishment and relief washing her face.

"Yeah. He got lightheaded and cranky, and just lost it. You know how he always skips breakfast, so I told him to start eating a big one, every day. You know, lots of bacon."

"Of course," her mother said, laughing. "He's a growing boy. Bacon it is! Well, let me see to that roast. He'll have a big plate of meat tonight!"

N. walked into the living room and turned on the TV. Tannara Stock was pouting over her shoulder into the camera, gyrating her rump at the same time. "This girl is a gift," she sang, "the one you want to open . . . "

N. stood up, turned her back to the TV and pouted over her shoulder. Tilting forward and thrusting out her rear end, she swung it side to side—just once—and felt the crinkle of the forgotten letter in her pocket. Flustered, she quickly sat back down and clicked off the TV, her face burning. Surely *she* couldn't have done something so stupid as to wiggle her butt around. Thank goodness no one had seen.

She pulled out the letter. Why had Mr. Slanger written to Emmet? She hesitated—barely—then slid her fingers inside the unsealed envelope and pulled out a single piece of paper.

This message is for Emmet Marcona.

She was his sister. Right now, that was as close to Emmet as Slanger was going to get.

I know how it is between a boy and his father. My dad deserted me, too. I've watched you in the woods, and know the rage that burns in your heart. The woods are a good place to hide, but nothing remains hidden forever. If you want to talk, come to the clearing, the one past Doug Bracken's house, one night next week. Halloween would be good. We often show ourselves best when we wear a mask, whether real or imagined. I'll be waiting.

Don't be afraid of the dark, Emmet. The night can tell you who you are.

Sincerely,
Nicholas Slanger

And, scrawled across the bottom of the page—

I know how it is for a boy who needs to spread his wings.

Emmet Marcona
Tomington Center—Wing A—Dr. Milton
Assignment
November 12

Yes, I dream sometimes. The strangest one? It was the same day I was accused of biting Jeff Johnson, after Mom drove me home and I fell asleep in my room. I was walking through the woods on the path behind Doug Bracken's house, moving toward Mr. Slanger's place.

It was daytime, but the air was dark somehow. Maybe it was dawn, or dusk. I'm not sure. I saw something out of the corner of my eye. A fox! I turned to look, but instead of a fox, I saw a woman. A lot older than me, but somehow young. <u>Beautiful</u>. Wrapped in a mossy green cloak, with a gauntlet on her wrist. She had red hair, darker than Niki's— more like your own, actually—and bright, sparkling eyes. Her lips parted, and she looked at me and laughed.

Then she tossed something upward from her wrist— a hawk of some kind. It shrieked, and I watched it flap awkwardly, its wings hugely wide, gaining composure and strength as it struggled through the air, rising between branches and leaves of trees, finally disappearing into the sky above. Amazed, I turned to the woman again. She was gone.

Then Niki walked into my room and woke me up. Just like she says in her story.

Living so close to the woods, I've seen plenty of hawks in the sky, so it's not strange, really, that I dreamed of one. I don't know why I dreamed about a fox, or a hawk, or a beautiful woman.

It wasn't an omen or anything.

I walk and watch the sky. Or did, before I became trapped in this room. Sometimes I saw Slanger. Sometimes I spoke to him. Except it's more like he talked to me. He's a famous author, so I listened, thinking he might tell me something I needed to hear.

"Truth is nothing but a lie manipulated into art," he said. "Look at your father, look at your sister."

That day, the day of the dream, Niki parked herself on my quilt as if she owned me, owned my bed, owned my room, and was free to possess all of it, run her fingers over all of it.

I was hungry, so she offered to get me something to eat. She brought back a plate of bologna. No bread. No mayonnaise or mustard. Just naked bologna. Sat there and grinned while I ate it.

Is that crazy or what? <u>She's</u> the one in trouble.

I wish she'd pay attention to her own life, instead of mine. Keep both feet in reality, not just one. But she never listens. She always thinks there's something better than real life going on—she just has to find it. At least she didn't get upset about what happened with Jeff Johnson, like Mom did. That's one good thing about Niki—everything is just another element in her story, the great fantasy she's weaving in her head.

Like the dream of family happiness.

She's convinced Dad will come home. She won't say it out loud, but she's always believed he'll come home.

He's gone, Niki. He's never coming back.

From: Douglas Bracken <dougman@minimen.com>
To: Dr. Rita I. Milton <Milton@tellet.com>
Sent: Tuesday, November 12—5:30 PM
Subject: The Truth

Dr. Milton,

Thanks for calling me last night! I'm glad Dad realized it was you and not another nutcase or fart-head reporter. He always tells me to be polite, but I guess sometimes a person just has to yell. He knows a lot more cuss words than I realized. Total calls received between Sunday and Monday: 46.

I agree with you that the truth is important, but my English teacher says that the truth is often painful. Do you agree? As a psychiatrist, you probably see more than your share of the dregs of humanity, so you might not like to talk about it too much. I'll understand if you prefer to remain silent.

Yes, I turned in a piece for the Father Project--a poem about my father and Fiona. I'd send it to you, but other than Niki, no one else has read it yet. I want to keep it a secret, so it will be a surprise for Dad when it actually gets published. It turned out really good!

And thank you for telling me about your son. I'm really sorry he died, though I guess it happened a few years ago. Still, that's just awful! Did they ever catch the guy who killed him? I mean, yikes. I know what it's like to lose someone, though the only thing violent about my mother's death was what the cancer did to her. You didn't mention having a husband, but Dad says that life without a partner is sorry indeed, so maybe getting one would help you feel better.

As for the truth about Niki and Emmet, I think being depressed can make you do things, like pretend you're an animal. When my mother died, all I wanted to do was curl up like a hedgehog and hide. That's pretty much what I did. I stayed in bed a <u>lot</u>. Then Dad said we had to move on, that Mom would want us to continue with our lives. So I stopped being a hedgehog. I think Niki and Emmet have just taken it a little further. I've never seen Emmet turn into a hawk! And Niki likes to tease. Being a cat would be a good choice, though. You could sleep all day!

Seriously, I think it's just their way of handling stuff.

As for Halloween, maybe going for a walk in the woods at night was a stupid idea. I think that's the main problem here. I'm sure I just saw a bunch of bushes and trees that looked like Mr. Slanger. It was pretty spooky out.

I have to stop now, and fix dinner. Have you ever had French toast for supper? I'm thinking that might be the way to go, since I forgot to take the ground beef out of the freezer this morning before I left for school, and we finished up the hot dogs last night. (Dad's had indigestion for two days, I think from all the phone calls. Maybe the dogs didn't help.)

Speaking of school, since Sunday's TV show, everyone is being very mean about Niki and Emmet. I won't repeat some of the things I've heard, as they are basically X-rated. I mean, really. Niki and Emmet <u>doing</u> stuff? That's totally disgusting. And not true!

Doug Bracken
"Calm in the eye of the psychiatric storm"

I just made that up. You can use it if you want. No charge!

Messenger-boy gave me the toy mouse you sent. Is this some kind of joke? I gave up stuffed animals a long time ago.

Look, you can try to cuddle up to Emmet if you like (good luck!) but it won't work with me. If you want to help Emmet, send him home.

So, Dr. Milton, how's life at Psycho Central? Getting cozy with the staff, are you? I really think Weasel-face is too young for you. I mean, you've got this fat-butt degree, and he can't be much older than his early twenties. Of course, he does have that degree in delivery service. That's gotta get some people hot.

By the way, I've been rummaging through my father's old newspaper columns. Guess what! He interviewed you for an article two and a half years ago, when Tomington lost its bid to expand and add a wing. Guess the locals don't like the locos!

So, how did you and Dad hit it off?

Intrigue Surrounds Slanger Investigation

by Carl Brenner
Mid-State News staff writer

GANTON—Though Nicholas Slanger remains missing, Chief Wilkinson refuses to speculate on the nature of his personal life. Was he really the hermit most people believed he was?

At yesterday's press conference, a woman named Belinda McGee stepped forward, shouting to Chief Wilkinson that Slanger was known to visit a strip club in nearby Harden City. When questioned by reporters after the conference, McGee, a comely woman of 31, admitted that she was a dancer at the Kitten's Den, and had seen Slanger there on more than one occasion. According to her, Slanger even paid her for a private dance.

A call to Victor Fitz, manager of the Kitten's Den, revealed that while McGee had indeed worked there in the past, she had been fired, for reasons he wouldn't specify. "The woman's a publicity seeker and a menace," Fitz said, adding, "I have never once seen Nicholas Slanger in this establishment, and neither has anyone else."

McGee, when contacted, said she would be talking to her lawyer about Fitz's remarks.

THE FATHER PROJECT

Chapter Five

The boy sat at the kitchen table across from his sister, staring at the ceramic hound-dog salt- and pepper shakers. "A weekend at home won't hurt you, Em," their mother said, as she poked and turned the bacon sizzling in the frying pan. N.'s nose twitched at the dense, heavy smell of cooked meat—it would fill her stomach, but not please.

"I'm glad you're feeling better," her mother continued. "You certainly look a little better, but you still need to rest. And"—she triumphantly lifted several strips of bacon out of the pan with a fork—"eat!" She seemed to believe she'd discovered the answer to all their problems: Emmet was underfed! He was a growing boy! He needed more food! That's why he'd had that little episode.

N., who had gotten up at the crack of dawn to slip out of the house on a little cat business—the dew against her nose a delicious intoxication—had successfully hunted and eaten a mole. Not much, a preliminary, early meal, breakfast #1, but—wait, what was that? A movement outside the window caught her eye just as she slipped another chunk of raw bacon under the table to Emmet.

She leaned to look. *Hmm.* The black cat her mother had mentioned. It was full-grown, rough-looking, big, and undisputedly male. Homeless, no doubt. N. watched as it crouched among the fallen leaves on the back lawn, devouring the head off a squirrel. She'd never caught anything that large. An entire *squirrel!* Her muscles twitched excitedly. Hiding in the brush, she'd once seen Emmet snare a rabbit, sinking his talons into its body to carry it up, but he'd lost his grip and dropped it. Amazingly, the rabbit had scampered away.

This squirrel wasn't going anywhere.

Emmet bumped her leg with his foot, a slipper sock keeping him safe from actual touch, and she gave him the last of the filched bacon. Raw bacon wasn't exactly the same thing as raw meat, but it was something.

She watched him stuff it in his mouth and hurriedly chew. He *did* look better. Should she show him the letter from Slanger? She felt a strange apprehension dance across her skin, like fur being stroked the wrong way. Why had he written to Emmet at all? Their family business was no concern of his. And how did he know about *wings*?

"I talked to Aunt Tam again last night," their mother said, as she spread the last of the bacon out on a paper towel to drain. "She said—"

She cleared her throat and reached for the carton of eggs.

"Well, ever since your father"—her voice broke and she paused a moment—"well, I mean, it's been a long time, now. And I—"

She broke the eggs into a bowl, whipping them with a fork. "Well, Aunt Tam thinks I haven't really been up-front with you. And she's right, I haven't."

She turned to face N. and Emmet, smiling a little too brightly. "I've met someone. A man. He makes me happy. And I want you to meet him."

N. sat, shocked into silence. Then, hairs prickling up the back of her neck, "You've met someone?"

"Yes," her mother said, turning deliberately to pour the eggs into the frying pan. "I'm not going to live the rest of my life alone. Your father certainly isn't."

"But if Dad's come back—"

"If he's come back—and we don't really know that he has—he's still made no attempt to contact us, not even to talk to *you*, his own children. And as for me, well, I've found someone new."

Emmet's eyes, troubled and muddied, locked on N. A tiny hiss escaped her lips.

"Anyway, it's time you met him. I know it's a lot all at once, so I've invited Aunt Tam and Uncle Arnie to dinner tomorrow, along with cousin Melody. And"—she took a deep breath, her voice shaking slightly—"my new friend." She stirred the pan. "It's time we got on with our lives. I think you'll like him."

N. bared her teeth at her mother's back.

"And if you don't—well, not everything in life turns out the way you want it to. Which is something I've had to learn over the past two years. But we can all be polite." She turned to set a plate piled high with bacon, eggs, and toast in front of Emmet. "Right?"

N. forcibly retracted her nails under the table. "Right." She smiled bitterly. Maybe her mother was ready for a new man, but that didn't mean she and Emmet were! If her father came back—

She squeezed her eyes shut. What would she do?

She opened her eyes. Slowly, deliberately, she made herself a scrambled egg and bacon sandwich and looked out the window. The black cat was gone, leaving just the headless carcass of the squirrel.

Animal justice, ruthless and swift. And totally satisfying.

Emmet sat on his bed, legs crossed, his face turned to the window, his unhappiness tucked away and hidden. N. knew he wanted to be outdoors, wanted to carve his anguish in the sky—but he'd been grounded and was obeying their mother. A bird of prey lived, without question, by the laws of nature. Emmet, in his human form, lived, without question, by the blunt laws laid down for him by human genome and human habit. Except he'd broken those rules Friday. He'd changed—just barely stopping himself—when he wasn't supposed to, when he would have been exposed.

Beak Boy.

N., sitting at his desk, looked away from him. *Danger!* sang through her veins like a cold rain. Their mother had betrayed them by finding someone new. And, just as important, a new person coming into their life would increase their chances of being found out. That couldn't happen.

She turned on Emmet's computer. She had one of her own, but

what she needed wasn't on hers. Besides, while she liked being alone, she also liked company, even if the feeling wasn't reciprocated. Emmet was company. She watched his head move slightly as he followed a bird drifting across the sky above the trees. She knew he'd rather be up there himself—gliding, soaring, and looking down. Sighting something far below, and plunging for the kill.

"I'm getting on," she said. He barely nodded. She knew all his passwords, all his programs. He didn't care about his computer, and only used it if he had to, for school. He didn't care about anything technological, hadn't even pestered their mother for a driver's license. Face it, he would never find what he needed in a car or online. There was no such thing as a satisfying virtual meal. Not once your heart has shrieked with the joy of the hunt. Not once blood, fresh and hot, has bathed your tongue.

She went into his address book. After they'd started their transformation, they'd pretty much fallen away from their friends, online and off. What was the point? The world was filled with people who knew nothing.

Doug Bracken, though, had never understood he wasn't necessary. He continued to send Emmet e-mail, chattering away on the bus and casting embarrassed, hopeful glances in N.'s direction. To N., he'd only been an annoying neighbor and a useless boy. Now, though, she needed his address. She paused, feeling the pain of an absent tail; she wanted to twitch it back and forth. Maybe now he would be a useful boy.

Hey Doug. guess what? my mom has bf. weird, huh? she's inviting him to dinner tomorrow. since u know all about the parental-dating scene, maybe u can give us some advice? u can come to Sunday dinner, eat, provide back-up, etc. I wouldn't know what to say to this guy. heh. :)   also, i need to ask u some questions about the clearing in the woods behind yr house.

Slanger had told Emmet to meet him there—at night—but she couldn't explain that to Doug.

---

lmk if u can come. :)

She added her own address and hit Send. "I invited Doug," she informed Emmet.

He turned slowly to face her.

"To the dinner tomorrow," she added. "He's pretty smart. He'll help us figure this guy out."

Emmet nodded slightly and turned back to the window.

N. stretched, tired from being up so early. She crossed the room and tentatively eased herself onto Emmet's bed. He glanced at her, frowning, his eyes focused and tight. She curled up beside him on his quilt, careful not to touch. He let her stay, flicking his eyes back to the window. As her thoughts turned pleasantly dim and gray, the heat from his body radiated outward. She sought it like radar, sleepily rearranging herself till she touched. *Joy!* Emmet tensed, but didn't move away. That was fair, she reasoned, giving space to human thought before she slept. Hadn't she fed him beef and bacon?

Emmet continued to watch the sky. N.'s eyes, half open, finally shut.

Using a rag, N. gingerly picked up the headless squirrel by its tail and carried it toward the small patch of woods behind their house. Suburbia, petering out at this point, gave itself up entirely just past the Pig Pie Diner. Then the woods ruled. Slanger's woods.

She'd never seen him. And for sure didn't care about his stupid books.

N. stood still, holding the squirrel upside down. She had never really considered the link between their place and Slanger's before—never had a reason to. If you knew which path to pick through the thickening trees and brush, you could probably walk from their skinny patch of woods to his big one, without ever once using the road.

Emmet, of course, could take the fastest route—straight through the sky. Had Slanger looked up one day and seen a hawk gliding above the trees? How would he have known it was a boy, transformed?

N. moved toward the woods. She had new worries on her mind. What would her mother's friend be like? Would he find them out?

She swung her arm and sent the squirrel flying, watching as it sailed past tree trunks and disappeared into a cluster of vines and shrub.

A movement in the yard caught her eye. A black shape, low to the ground, streaked across the grass and into the woods. N. frowned. That black cat again.

Wow. It's so gr8 to hear from u ... I'd love to come to dinner ... Dad's working tomorrow so I'm on my own. I know all about parents dating and stuff. Oh, and I know the woods. Guess what?!?!?! I've started my poem about Dad and Fiona. I only have one stanza so far:

> One night at the Pig Pie Diner,
> My dad, a widower, ordered the steak platter,
> Which comes with fries. "That hostess," he said,
>   "sure is finer
> Than any woman who can matter,
> Except my wife, who I still pine-fer,
> But now I'm older and lonely and fatter."

What do ya think? Let me know. cya 2morrow—Doug

Emmet Marcona
Tomington Center—Wing A—Dr. Milton
Assignment
November 13

You still wonder if Niki is really the author of "The Father Project?" Who else could it be? Not Mom, I can assure you, even if she did once win a prize. Even if she is frustrated with her life. Mom would never expose our family like Niki has—she would never embarrass us that way.

Niki doesn't know embarrassment.

You have to understand that she's a storyteller, and always has been. That's how she lives in the world, how she survives. Yes, I've worried that she can't always tell what's real from what isn't. I tried to watch out for her when I was at home. In truth, though, Niki mostly watched me. Mom doesn't really understand what Niki is like—how she takes what she wants, and uses it for her own ends. How she's impossible to tame.

Has Mom spoken to you recently? I still haven't heard from her. I thought she would have sent me a card by now. I know she's busy, though. Thank you for giving me the stuffed animal from Niki. It's like her to do that—send me something goofy.

Please tell her that I like it. I wish I could tell her myself—but you've asked me not to write to her just now, and I don't have access to a phone. Anyway, the mouse is sitting on my pillow, looking at me. It's embarrassing to admit this, but now I don't feel so alone.

Reading her story, I have to admit, is painful—and surprising. She gets everything wrong, of course. But I don't see that as a sickness. She's just creative. Niki doesn't lie, she simply rearranges the truth.

She's correct that Mom grounded me after the so-called "biting" incident—but it's not like I'm the only kid who's ever had to stay home.

Still, being grounded for a day made me realize that I had to show Mom I was okay, not crazy or anything. So that night, Saturday, I sat on the couch with her and Niki and watched a movie. And it worked—Mom was happy, or seemed to be. Maybe she wanted us to look like a regular family, able to welcome a new person into the fold.

I admit I dreaded the dinner she'd arranged. I really didn't want to meet her boyfriend, but knew I needed to act the part. Pretend to be a good, attentive son, happy for his mother's new life. Pretend I didn't want to leave.

Anyway, that night I sat at one end of the couch, Niki in the middle. I put a cushion upright between us, pretending to use it as an armrest, so she wouldn't touch me. She was leaning against Mom, though, who stroked her arm and head as if she were a little kid. She _is_ a little kid, inside.

The movie was one of those natural disaster flicks. An earthquake hits New York City, tons of people die, the hero lives. Blah blah. Movies like that are all the same. Mom loves them, though, maybe because our family turned into a natural disaster when Dad left, and this allows her to work it out. Or something.

I think our family was a disaster before Dad left. Niki only remembers the good parts about Mom and Dad—like the way Dad would sneak up behind Mom when she was cooking and kiss her on the back of the neck, making her giggle. Yes, that happened. In the movies, when the husband has an affair, they always say it's because the wife is frigid or something. But I don't think that was the case. Maybe Mom began to notice that, with Dad, she came in second behind Niki. _I_ liked Mom. But she didn't see me.

Mom loved Dad, though, and maybe she wishes I was the one who'd left instead of him. But it's natural, I think, for a woman to prefer her husband over her son.

I'll tell you something.

Dad's focus was always on _people_—talking to them, writing about them in the _Frontier_. As if he was everybody's best friend. But he didn't have any friends. Not real ones. His closeness to others was all through words.

But his charm won everybody over. He focused it on ordinary people, moving through their extraordinary lives. He actually said that in one of his columns. Take any plain-Jane rock and polish it, and you'll find a gem. He said that, too. Everyone was so happy to have his attention, they never noticed that the only one he was truly connected to was Niki.

I noticed.

It confused me. I thought he should be paying more attention to Mom, or even to me. Maybe that's why I started spending so much time in the woods. Being alone calmed me.

Solitude is best, after all. See, you can't truly study nature—trees or insects or animals, or the sky—if you're around someone else all the time, talking. You can't see anything, either. Once, just inside a small clearing in the woods, a ways behind Doug Bracken's house, I saw something glinting under a pile of dried, brown leaves. Reaching down, I picked up a knife, lovely and old and strange, with an odd design on the handle. Maybe it belonged to Gypsies!

No. Just kidding. It was an ordinary kitchen knife, the kind that's sharp.

The point is, I never would have seen it, if I'd been with my father, or even with a friend. Your eyes are everything. Maybe that's why I've given up on talking.

Sometimes I wonder if Dad felt a strangeness at times, like something was pushing outward from his skin, as if wings were forming. A cry for freedom, urging him to go. How much can you blame a man, for finally answering his own loneliness, his own wildness?

So, I'm supposed to sit in this house for the rest of my life, while you keep Emmet a prisoner? Sorry, but I already have someone missing, Dad. Seems like you've spent more time than I like with both of them.

So how come you won't answer my question about my father?

By the way, I think messenger-boy's had plastic surgery. I think the face he's wearing is not his own. There are odd little stretches and tucks here and there. Is he an ex-con or something? Covering up a murder, maybe? Inquiring minds want to know. Not too many people try to make themselves look more like a weasel.

Why do you keep sending him, anyway? Are you afraid to meet me in person?

Alright, Milton, fess up. Q & A time. What do you know about Dad? Anything? Nothing?

Break your phony psychiatric silence and SPEAK.

Disappearance a Prank?

by **CARL BRENNER**
Mid-State News staff writer

GANTON—A woman identifying herself as Nicholas Slanger's ex-wife has stepped forward, saying that Slanger was known to play pranks.

The woman, Sandra Fairly, recalled that fifteen years ago, when she and Slanger were still married, he rented a coffin for a Halloween-night party. Setting the coffin in their living room, he then produced an actual cadaver, which he had secreted away from a medical school. Dressing it in ghoulish attire, he placed it in the coffin.

The guests, as well as Fairly, who has since remarried, thought it was a cleverly made-up mannequin until someone reached into the coffin to playfully tickle the "dead person" on the tummy.

The party ended immediately, leading, Fairly believes, to the rapid close of Slanger's social life, and to the end of their marriage.

However, Fairly was not able to offer proof of their marriage, and *Mid-State News* can find no one who can corroborate her claims.

In his most recent press conference, Chief Wilkinson advised people to "not believe everything they read, and to not jump to conclusions." Finn Tyler, a regular at the Pig Pie, said, "The only conclusion I'm jumping to is that the Chief doesn't have one idea worth a rat's [posterior] about what's really going on."

THE FATHER PROJECT

Chapter Six

The girl ignored the light, bouncy soft rock coming from the radio. Why did people subject themselves to such endless, useless noise? Grimacing, she carried a stack of her mother's good dinner plates to the table. Let's see, Aunt Tam and Uncle Arnie, and their daughter, cousin Melody, made three. She and Emmet and Doug and her mother made seven. And her mother's boyfriend—eight.

Boyfriend and Doug weren't here yet. Melody was in the bathroom, making herself even more gorgeous than she already believed she was. N. growled softly, setting the plate with the tiny chip on its edge in Melody's spot.

Satisfied, she finished setting the table.

Wandering into the living room, she ignored both the music and her aunt and uncle, heading directly to the card table in the corner, set up as a makeshift bar. Standing behind it, parked at a safe distance, was Emmet, in dress pants and a white shirt, ready to pour, as requested, ginger ale or Coke or 7-Up into plastic cups. For those needing a little something more, wine was available. Their mother's crystal wineglasses, bright and shiny, stood upright and waiting to be filled.

N., too, wore her best clothing—a soft, velvety light blue dress. Combing her hair before coming downstairs, she'd looked at herself carefully in the mirror: red-gold hair that touched her shoulders, pale blue eyes, slight figure. Short. Not exactly pretty, not exactly plain.

No animal except human would tolerate such apparel.

Her mother was talking to Aunt Tam and Uncle Arnie a little too loudly, her face bright with both excitement and anxiety. She had on her forest-green dress, which, N. had to admit, complemented both her complexion and her dark hair. N. smiled. *She* was the only redhead in the family.

She watched her mother hand a photograph to Aunt Tam. When had she been meeting with Boyfriend? *Ah.* PTA meetings. Her mother had announced an unusual number of them recently. That must be it—she'd been lying and sneaking. N. stared at her mother. Humans pursued love so blithely, as if there were no consequences.

There were always consequences.

R-ring!

N. jumped, her heart pounding. No one ever used the doorbell. Willing her heart to slow down, she watched her mother open the front door. A man, taller and thinner than her father, stepped inside, a hopeful light in his eyes. A warning growl rose in N.'s throat. Boyfriend had arrived.

N. watched from across the room as Boyfriend was introduced to her aunt and uncle, the music covering their words. She stood faithfully beside Emmet as Boyfriend and her mother approached the card table. Whatever else they were, she and Emmet were a team. She glanced at him, his face drained of color.

Her mother bit her lip slightly, her eyes bright. "Honey, Emmet, I want you to meet my friend, Nick."

Nick? Oh, please. They had to have the same name? Faking a smile, she thrust her hand forward, giving Emmet time to prepare. Tight with anxiety, he finally held out his hand, too, wincing as Boyfriend took it.

"Great to meet you kids." He beamed. "I've heard so much about you." He laughed. "Good things!"

"Wine?" N.'s mother asked.

"Sure," Boyfriend said, smiling at N. She faked another smile. Maybe that's why her mother hadn't mentioned his name before—too much competition among the N.s. Well, who cared, really?

She glanced at Emmet's unhappy face, his hands trembling as he poured his mother and Boyfriend each a glass before they strolled back to the couch. N. cooed softly, trying to calm her brother, his human heart as fragile as a baby bird's.

"We'll be fine," she said. "He's harmless." Emmet only shut his eyes, worry and confusion racing across his face. Was he too far gone to understand that this man meant nothing, that nothing human meant anything to them anymore? Not even their father. *Damn him!* She clenched her hands into fists. She'd been much happier before her father had returned. If he had. No way would he claim her heart again!

Love was such a human torment. Transformation had set them free.

Melody approached the table and N.'s nails sharpened, then retracted—she'd always hated her cousin. Three years older than N., tall and slender, she wore chic Junkie slacks and an expensive white Welfare blouse. Her pretty face carefully made up, she looked like a supermodel, minus some of the super. Emmet sent one long but confused and startled look at her across the room, then latched his eyes and hands onto the ice bucket.

"Hi, guys," Melody said, launching a heat-seeking missile of a smile directly at Emmet, her short, dark hair feathered like angel silk around her face.

Didn't Melody know Emmet was her *cousin*? Six-fingered children, anyone?

"Mind pouring me a little something?" Melody asked, sparkling her eyes at Emmet, completely ignoring N. She waved the empty plastic cup she was holding. "7-Up gets pretty dull after a while." She eyed the wine bottle.

Emmet froze, unable to move.

"Have some Coke," N. suggested, upending the large plastic bottle and sending a torrent of dark liquid into Melody's glass, splashing it all over her hand. N. forced her nails to remain blunt. Still, one swipe and—

"So what are *you*?" Melody sneered, her eyes narrow as she wiped her hand on a napkin. "The drink police?"

Hearing the front door open, N. glanced up. Doug.

"Hi! Sorry I'm late." Doug, flushed and out of breath, rushed across the room, eyes focused only on her. Banging into the table, he knocked over an empty wineglass. "Oh, gosh. Sorry." Attempting to pick it up, he overturned another. "Darn." He got them upright, his face turning a deeper red as N. slid them out of his reach. He clapped one hand over his nose just as a volcanic sneeze erupted.

N. handed him a napkin. Had he run the whole way to her house? A needless expenditure of energy. That was just so human.

He finished wiping and sniffed. "I think I'm catching a cold." He tucked the napkin in his pocket. "I'm late because I was making a macaroni-and-cheese casserole for Dad. He'll need something to eat when he gets home tonight. I also left a can of peas out on the counter. You'd think—"

His words died as he realized the tall, slender person standing next to him was not only a girl, but a girl who looked like a supermodel. His mouth opened and nothing came out.

A growl started to rumble up the back of N.'s throat. She hadn't invited Doug here to look at a human female *freak*.

N.'s mother hurried over to the table. "Honey, would you be a darling and check the roast? The potatoes are peeled and in the pot, ready to go—"

"Sure," N. said. "Relax and enjoy yourself." Maybe this relationship would turn out to be a good thing, distracting her mother's attention even more. Maybe she needed to encourage it.

Relieved, her mother smiled at Doug, patted Melody on the arm, then headed back to the adults. N. turned to go.

"I'll help," said Emmet, stepping on her feet in his panic to escape.

"We'll be back," N. announced, but Doug didn't seem to hear her. She watched him stare up at Melody, and watched Melody look down on him with amusement.

Stupid petty humans. She headed for the kitchen, her brother at her heels.

From: Douglas Bracken <dougman@minimen.com>
To: Dr. Rita I. Milton <Milton@tellet.com>
Sent: Thursday, November 14—9:04 PM
Subject: Bone

Dr. Milton, hi.

I saw on the news tonight (Channel 4 again--I have a hard time not watching Sadie Fuller. Does that make me a hypocrite?) that they found a bone in the woods! Right around the spot where we ended up that night. Right behind my house! (Well, not right behind. It's a good ways. You know that, don't you? It's not like all this stuff happened on my back porch.) Anyway, they think it's human. Do you know anything about it? What if somebody was murdered--I mean, <u>really</u> murdered--right nearby? I'm here by myself a lot.

They said it seemed to have been there a while, though, so it's probably not a piece of Mr. Slanger. If he's dead, I mean. They've sent it to forensics.

Dad told me not to think about the bone, as it will only give me nightmares. Well, I think I'm a little too old for nightmares! Except I can't stop thinking about it. And Mr. Marcona's been missing for a while, too. I seriously hope he's in France somewhere, enjoying his mistress.

What do you think will happen to the woods if Mr. Slanger really is dead? I hope somebody nice buys it, and they don't put up a Wal-Mart or a zillion townhouses. I worry about all the animals that live there. Maybe a rich Indian could come and buy it up and give it back to his tribe or something.

No, Mr. Slanger never gave me a letter to give to Emmet. But a while ago a woman found a piece of paper he'd dropped in the parking lot of the Pig Pie, which she turned in to the Lost and Found. It said something about birds and wings, probably notes for a book. I kind of filched it, figuring that was the closest I'd ever get to his autograph. I showed it to Emmet and Niki. They weren't real impressed, but they're not exactly fans of his, either.

From what I've read in the <u>Mid-State News</u>, Slanger sounds kind of porno. I asked Dad if he'd ever been to the Kitten's Den, and he said no. I'm not sure fathers always tell the truth about that kind of thing, though. It seems like everybody's got secrets.

Doug Bracken
"A poem or two will get us through
 The muck of life, its gunk and strife"

Emmet Marcona
Tomington Center—Wing A—Dr. Milton
Assignment
November 14

Yesterday you asked if I've ever had a "spell," or an "episode." What do you mean? Those words sound so old-fashioned, like something from a black-and-white movie, made a long time ago. Somebody going bonkers, killing people.

I'm not insane.

But, yes, there is a moment between doing something ordinary—like pouring soda into a plastic cup—and what I call <u>slipping away</u>. It's like exiting one space or dimension for another. Maybe it's a daydream, a place to go when something happens that's boring or upsetting, or that you know you'd get in trouble for, if anyone knew. A disturbance occurs—something changes shape or direction, maybe an electrical charge ignites the air—and you slip away.

It doesn't happen every day, and sometimes not for weeks or months at a time. Lately, though, it's been more often. Or was, before I came here.

This is how it goes: maybe I'll be walking by myself,

following one of the paths that meanders through the woods. Squirrels scamper through the trees, birds cry out—and suddenly I'll see Slanger, or remember Niki teasing me, poking at me, even though she knows I don't like to be touched—and that in-between moment arrives in a rush, some kind of turning in the air. I slip away, and find myself soaring in a kind of otherness. My muscles tense with a weird excitement, while my mind, both anxious and exhilarated, cramps, as if finding itself trapped in a small box. Though I can still see everything around me, I see it with different eyes, everything strangely distorted.

I'm both terrified and not, as if I'd been given a new body I don't yet know how to use, but somehow know is mine.

And then it ends. I'm back in my boy's body, standing still in the woods, my mouth dry, my heart pounding. Soon enough, I'm calm again, and continue my walk as if nothing had happened.

I've never told anyone.

Niki—if she knew—would call it some kind of magic, an incomplete transformation into something else. Me, I think it's just a hiccup, a physical reaction I can't avoid. The air changes, or time looks backward over its shoulder. I react and then it's gone.

The Saturday I was grounded—the one Niki mentions in her story—I sat on my bed, the window shade up as far as it would go, staring at the sky. Wanting to be in it, be a part of it. Yearning to be changed from my ordinary, common self. Suddenly that in-between moment was there, and I slipped into otherness. When I came back, Niki was parked on my quilt, legs crossed, staring at me, as if she'd somehow sensed I was gone and had come to my room to retrieve me. But how could she have known what happened to me? I've never told her.

Yet it's true that she wrote it in her story. As if she knew the temperature of my skin, the pulse of my heart. As if she'd been there with me.

Crazy.

That in-between moment almost happened the following day, too, at Mom's party. Melody came up to the table wanting a drink. She startled me, I think. I mean, she's my cousin, but I wasn't unaware of her body and the sex she was flaunting, just like models on TV. Sometimes, even if the person doesn't interest you, the suggestion does, even if it frightens you. If that makes sense.

I started to slip—it's something I have no control over—but then I didn't. Maybe because Niki was there, pouring Coke all over Melody's hand. Disapproving. Wanting to direct the situation herself, shape it to her own satisfaction.

So many times at night—when I was home—as I fell asleep in my room, I would hear her typing away, writing one of her stories, one of her fantasies. She wants happy endings so badly, she writes them, again and again. But happy endings don't exist.

Okay. I got your message. Yes, two and a half years ago you gave my father an interview about Tomington. Big deal, ho-hum, snore. Words words words. But what else happened, Dr. Milton?

Weasel-boy might be watching me, but I'm watching you.

Watch. Watch.

But now, on to my story. This part is so cool!

We did it did it did it! Right upstairs while everybody else was downstairs, ignorant and stupid, drinking sodas and wine, yakking.

What if they had heard us? What if they had seen us? Delicious, delicious danger!

Pay attention, Dr. Milton, to what's going on in the world—so much more than you've imagined.

Bone Under Investigation

by **CARL BRENNER**
Mid-State News staff writer

GANTON—Police have not yet released any information about the bone found in the woods near the spot where the Halloween incident took place.

"It may take weeks for forensics to be able to tell us anything, as the bone is quite degraded from weather and, possibly, animal activity," Chief Wilkinson said at a press conference. "While it does appear to be human, it may have absolutely nothing to do with Nicholas Slanger's disappearance, or anyone else's."

The section of the woods where it was found has been cordoned off by police, but a walk along one of the many paths that wander through extended sections of the woods shows dense underbrush, thick trees, and an abundance of fallen leaves matted on the ground, all of which would make a search for other possible remains difficult. Wildlife does appear to be abundant. This reporter spotted a fox, a black snake, and a small, long-bodied animal that was later identified as a weasel.

Also spotted was a common house cat. Black, it scurried away, no doubt headed back to its bowl of milk in one of the houses that dot the edge of the woods.

THE FATHER PROJECT

Chapter Seven

The girl pulled the roast out of the oven, hoping her mother would be happy with rare. Rare wasn't as good as raw, but no one else would want raw.

Except Emmet.

He leaned against the counter, his brown hair gleaming under the fluorescent light. He looked bewildered, on the verge of tears. St. Nick couldn't be upsetting him *that* much.

N. set the roast on the counter. Maybe he was hungry.

Their mother, too distracted with cleaning the house and preparing the upcoming meal, hadn't cooked breakfast. Emmet had barely touched the bowl of cereal N. had handed him. Tired of bacon, he had refused to eat any that N. pushed into his palm, under the table, raw.

N. hadn't even been able to grab the plastic wrap that encased the uncooked roast and hand it to him to lick. Peeling it off the meat, their mother had immediately tossed it into the trash, then dumped coffee grounds on top. *Ugh.*

She rubbed grease off her fingers with a paper towel and looked at Emmet as he stared out the window. Why did his hands shake so? Surely Boyfriend—

She blinked, shocked. Maybe he wasn't upset about Boyfriend at all. Maybe it was *Melody*! She snarled, flattening her ears. Her brother didn't need some stupid human girl. He needed *her*.

A tickling notion teased her mind, and a quiet pleasure began to build in her limbs. With the noise of the company in the next room, perhaps this would be a good time for a little game. A harmless, playful pursuit. Something to distract him from their cousin.

"A meal is so important," she purred. "Especially when it's full of blood."

Emmet whipped his head around, hunger etching his face. The pupils in his eyes began to shift, and he looked at her as if from a great distance. N. felt her body grow soft and tense at the same time. Backing slowly away, she casually turned and strolled toward the other door in the kitchen, the one that opened to the back stairway leading to the second floor.

She paused there a moment, almost laughing, her mouth open, then leapt through the door just as Emmet's harsh cry filled her ears. Banging the door shut behind her, she tore up the stairs, energy pulsing through her arms and legs. As she ran, her body shrank, and her head and arms stretched forward until she was racing as if on four legs. And then she was. Her blue dress and flimsy underwear slid off behind her.

Transformed—her skin covered with a thick, delicious, light orange fur, her ears triangled up and forward, her teeth grown sharp in her mouth—she ran. The door below her crashed open, and she heard Emmet fill the stairway with a cold shriek. She ran faster, her muscles supple and strong, her heart charged with blood. He was almost upon her!

The doorway at the top of the stairs stood ajar. She slipped through expertly, knowing Emmet would have a harder time. Only half airborne—his legs and body shrinking, but not yet wholly bird—his clumsily expanding arms would push at the wooden barrier, trying to open it wider, fumbling. Still, though, he would come. She had only a few seconds to decide which way to go.

Their bedrooms were no good, the people below might hear. N. ran quickly down the hallway to the unlatched attic door and easily nudged it open with her front right paw. She slipped through, just as Emmet crashed into the hallway, his clothes falling away, his arms disappearing into awkward wings.

N. grinned to herself. He still couldn't get through a door with any grace. She slunk low on the steps leading up into the attic, taking them hurriedly. In a minute he'd be on her. She ran, sprinting to the top. Where to hide? Over there!

She changed direction, her momentum propelling her into a hapless slide across the floor. Crashing into an old trunk, she pulled herself upright, tail twitching in annoyance. How embarrassing! She had to work on her stops. Thank goodness no one had seen.

Suddenly the attic door at the bottom of the steps burst wide open. Her brother, his own transformation almost complete, struggled up the stairwell, then soared into the large, open attic, his wings wide—a majestic red-tailed hawk.

Death from the sky.

But he hadn't seen her yet! Using the trunk as a springboard, she leapt to the dusty shelf above, squeezing between an ancient hat box and a round tin of buttons, flattening down so just her nose and whiskers showed. Would he sense her, and look? Her heart raced with a pleasant terror and her muscles squeezed themselves deliciously tight. It was only a game, but—she waited, panting hotly, ears cocked.

Turning in the air, a flurry of mottled brown feathers, Emmet raked the almost empty attic with his eyes, his arms now an outrage of wings. He slowed to a careful swoop beneath the raftered ceiling, then settled below her on the banister that edged the open stairwell, folding his wings to his sides. His head turned slowly as each eye took in the dimly lit room. N. opened her mouth in a silent mewl.

She saw his talons dig into the wooden banister, and flexed her own small claws. He was below her at an angle. Once he was completely grown, his strength would be unmatched. But for now—she could take him. She could!

Her body started to tense, energy filling her legs till she ached to leap. It was just play—a little pounce, a little fun! She'd scare him, that's all. Startle him. What could be wrong? Her back legs started to bunch, preparing to leap. O glorious hunt!

Clutched to the shelf, she almost felt herself arc through the air—almost felt herself land on his back, sink her teeth into his neck, dig her claws through the feathers to find the meat of his body, ruining his wings. Almost.

Desire tightened her heart, giddiness rushing her head. Wasn't it her right, after all? Wasn't everyone someone else's prey? Energy throbbed in her limbs. She'd have him. It was her right. The hunt was hers. She'd have his blood!

A scuttle from the edge of the attic floor broke her concentration and she jerked back, knocking the tin of buttons to the floor. She cringed as it crashed open and buttons spilled everywhere across the wooden floor, finally twirling to a stop, their clatter and clicking whirl fading to a dusty silence.

She flattened back against the shelf, but now her brother, head turned in her direction, knew exactly where she was. She had to practice holding her positions! A growl escaped from her throat that quickly became a yowl. Frustrated, she flung herself off the shelf, crashing to the floor. Game over. She might as well change back.

With a shriek, Emmet dropped from the banister and bore down on her. *What!?* He couldn't! Their sacred rule!

But she felt his talons sink through the fur on her back, piercing the skin, the painful tug as he struggled to lift her off the floor. What was he doing? Terrified, she snarled and spit, trying to flail around and strike him on the leg. He had her blood!

His heavy wings beat hotly in the attic air as he struggled against her weight, his head darting to strike her with its sharp, curved beak. She wrestled, clawing at the air. Feeling a loosening of his grip, she twisted sharply and struck upward, scraping her claws across his face. Lucky hit! His talons opened in surprise.

She wriggled violently and landed on the floor with a thud, but he quickly blocked the stairway. She held her position, crouching low, hissing, her tail switching back and forth, her wound a burning pain in her back. He shook his head stupidly from the shock of being scratched, his beak open, his wide wings flapping awkwardly.

N. quickly peered around the room. If she didn't get away, he could strike and win her blood again—perhaps for good. The dusty windows admitted pale shafts of light. Only a single hook kept them shut. If she could get close enough to jump onto the sill, if she could work one open—

The scuttle sounded again, closer this time, and a terrified bundle of gray fur darted across the floor. A mouse! N. watched her brother flap back up into the air, his pain and awkwardness overcome by hunger, his attention fixed on the small lump of frightened rodent.

Mouse! N. wiggled her rear end, ready to leap, but Emmet bore down on the tiny animal with ease. He had its blood.

Ee-e-yow-w-w! The mouse should have been hers!

But even through her disappointment, her brain urgently signaled: *escape!* As Emmet tightened his talons around the squealing beast, she darted down the stairs and back through the attic door.

She fled down the hallway, her body growing in size once more, passing Emmet's clothing on the way, stumbling as her front legs turned back into arms and she found herself erect. Gaining her balance, she hurried down the steps toward the kitchen, the long tail that she so loved disappearing. She stopped before the kitchen door, shaking, and looked down at her body.

Human female. Breasts. *Naked.*

With trembling hands, she pulled on her silky underwear and slipped her blue dress over her head. Only the sore spots on her back, grown small and minor on her now much larger body, told the story of what had happened.

Her brother had taken her blood. And, with her scratch, she had taken his. Standing still, she breathed deeply, trying to calm herself. But her hands still shook.

They'd broken their sacred rule.

She stepped into the kitchen, where the fluorescent light glared. She washed her hands, then lifted the pot of peeled potatoes. Almost dropping it, water sloshing, she quickly set it back down.

They needed to talk.

Quietly, she ascended the stairs once more, walking down the hall-way past their bedrooms, tiptoeing up the dark, narrow steps that led to the attic. In the dim light she saw her brother, a large, frightened bird crouched on the banister, a drop of blood pearled between his feathers, above his eye.

She approached him, a soft, soothing sound like a purr coming from her throat, and he jerked back. She knew he would remain stuck in his bird shape a little longer, until the swallowed mouse worked its way a bit further into his belly. Eating in their changed state had its consequences.

"It's okay," she murmured, reaching with her fingers and stroking his breast, spotted now with tiny flecks of blood. He drew back and opened his mouth in distress, but she persisted, tucking her finger under his beak and pulling it upward.

She stared, mesmerized by the drop of blood. Not thinking, she leaned forward until her lips were close. Gently, she touched her tongue to his wound. The taste of his blood sprang open in her mouth, like a brilliant red box. She pulled away, dizzy, as he struggled against her forced intimacy.

Hunger roared in her gut. She pushed her nails beneath his feathers, tightening her fingers around his neck, longing to twist it hard, knowing she could crush his head, make his blood completely hers. A terrible pleasure ran through her body. She wanted this! He'd never look at Melody again—or at anyone else.

He didn't struggle against her grip. Why? His talons could easily pierce her skin. But he sat as still as if he were broken and caged—resigned to his fate. Joy rushed her limbs—his life was hers! But his golden eyes still gleamed with something familiar. Puzzled, she stared—and for a moment saw her own too-human eyes reflected back. Startled, she dropped her hands, stunned, remembering. He was her *brother*.

"Hey! Anybody there?" Doug's voice floated up from the hallway. "Where are you guys?"

Horrified, she backed away from Emmet, then turned and ran down the steps.

Emmet Marcona
Tomington Center—Wing A—Dr. Milton
Assignment
November 15

I'm tired of taking the pills you give me. What are
they supposed to do, besides make me sleepy?
Sometimes I think they're not real medication at
all. Does Mom know about them? I bet she'd tell
you to stop giving them to me. I wish she'd come
visit. I know, I know—she's busy. She'd come if she
could.

Did you think these pills would make me talk? Dr.
Milton, I'm entitled to some choices. Everything isn't
<u>you</u>.

Even if I did talk, I'm not sure you'd listen. You look
at me funny sometimes, as if—well, as if you
already know everything there is to know about me,
all my habits and weaknesses, and are waiting to
pounce. A lot like Niki.

Dr. Milton, I'm not just some kind of project that
everybody's working on. I'm real.

But, to answer your question, yes, Niki scratched me,
and it happened pretty much the way she said—
only, of course, <u>not</u> the way she said.

The dinner party was going on, and Mom asked her
to check the roast. I tagged along, mostly, I think, to

get away from Melody. I already told you how she affected me.

Also, I admit I felt kind of weird about Mom's boyfriend. About them being together. I mean, I know I'm not supposed to be jealous. I'm her son, not her husband. We were never like Niki and Dad.

And I know Mom deserves someone new, just like everybody else. It's just—I wish someone besides Niki wanted to be with me. Is that so horrible?

Anyway, right after Niki took the roast out, sticking it with a fork, she dragged me all the way up to the attic to help her dig something out of a trunk— she didn't even tell me what she was looking for. Then when we got there, she turned and jumped me—she still had the fork—and scratched me above the eye, under my eyebrow. She could have put my eye out!

Then she ran back downstairs. I just sat on the step, dumbfounded.

A couple of minutes later, she crept back up full of apology, examining my eye and kissing me on the forehead, as if I were a little kid. Then Doug called from the hallway below, and she hurried back down.

I'm not sure she was really sorry for what she did. Maybe she was acting out one of her crazy fantasies. She's too old for that, though. It hurt! I bleed like everybody else.

Maybe Niki thinks I don't have feelings. Look, I might be a loner, but that doesn't mean I don't have feelings. I have lots of feelings! She just gets me all mixed up somehow, pushing me. She doesn't know about limits and boundaries. But she's my younger sister. I'm supposed to protect her.

I've tried, honestly.

Yesterday you asked me about guilt—though I don't know what I'm supposed to feel guilty about—and almost put your hand on my head. You pulled back, remembering, I guess, how I feel about being touched.

It's just that I know what it can do to you. Make you feel human. Make you feel—like you've not really human at all. Like you've done something wrong.

If you had touched me—I admit, I almost wish you had—who would I have been at that moment? A crazy person, or just a teenage boy, separated from his family? I honestly don't know. Who did you want me to be? Even doctors have feelings. A patient? Or something different? The way you look at me sometimes—

Well, it's not unlike the way Niki looks at me. Like I'm everybody's prey.

I can't bear it when I feel so confused. That's why I didn't mind sitting on the attic step the day that Niki scratched me—it centered me somehow. Calmed me. Even though an attic is the opposite, really, of the sky. The sky is endless, open—a constant newness, a distance you can never cross. An attic is entirely enclosed, a set number of square feet, a space holding things not used anymore, things passed down from one person to another and finally discarded. Clothes and books belonging to dead people.

Sometimes I wonder if my father is dead. Not just gone, but dead. As if death were the only way to escape his own skin, his own guilt, the mess of our family.

At times, even now, when I wake up early in the morning, when everything is silent and still—just like in the attic—I almost think I can hear him calling me. It's not a voice, exactly. It's more like something in the atmosphere, a movement or turning in the air, tugging at me. Telling me, <u>Emmet, it's time. Wake up.</u> As if, in this altered state, he can finally talk to me without disliking me so, as if he can give me direction, or even love me.

It's a challenge to become my true self, I think—a loner moving through the world without attachment. A hunter of solitude.

But as much as I long to leave, <u>need</u> to leave, I'm also frightened.

Sometimes—okay, I admit it—I feel safe here, on Wing A. I'm enclosed. I have blankets to wrap myself in. Nobody touches me.

From: Douglas Bracken <dougman@minimen.com>
To: Dr. Rita I. Milton <Milton@tellet.com>
Sent: Friday, November 15—4:01 PM
Subject: Dreams

Dear Dr. Milton,

Dad told me you called last night. Sorry I was in bed and couldn't talk--I don't usually crash so early, but I was really upset. Did you see Channel 4 news? Sadie Fuller gave a "Special Update," and said --I can't believe she said it right out loud!--that someone had called the station to report that Niki and Emmet were having an "incestuous relationship." That's sick! I mean, that's what all the kids on the bus keep saying, but I thought reporters <u>reported</u>, not just repeated cheap, stupid gossip. And who made the call, anyway? "Unnamed source," ha!

It's so unfair! Niki and Emmet aren't like that at all. Niki's blunt and outspoken, sure, and Em's kind of quiet and sensitive, but that doesn't exactly make them porno! I can't stand it. I miss them both. I hate riding the bus when everybody's talking about them, spreading disgusting lies. I tried to call Emmet again last night, but they wouldn't put my call through. Why won't you let him talk? I think it would help him, Dr. Milton. And Mrs. Marcona won't let Niki anywhere near the phone, either, and all my e-mails bounce right back. I know everything's a mess, but I'm still their friend.

Dad keeps telling me to calm down, but he's the one who ate the entire package of Chips Ahoy cookies last night. I didn't get even one! But he wants me to cooperate with you--he says that's how I can help Niki and Em. So, okay then. If it will help.

You asked about dreams. Well, right now I feel like I'm living inside a nightmare. Other than that, I'd like to be a famous poet someday. Or maybe a police investigator, like Chief Wilkinson. Everybody keeps telling us we're supposed to dream big.

But maybe you mean night dreams? I dream about my mother sometimes. Do you think she might be jealous of Fiona? I worry about that. It'd be terrible to want my father to get married again, then find out later that my mother was really pissed.

She was never one to stay angry, though. She was really nice. She could make like sixteen different kinds of hamburgers. Regular, Hawaiian, South-of-the-Border--too many to name. They all had different seasonings, different condiments. She served the South-of-the-Border with chili sauce, the Hawaiian with grilled pineapple slices. Each one had its own flavor. They all tasted great, though, with ketchup. So far, I've only made Regular, served with pickles and potato chips. As a matter of fact, that's what we're having tonight.

Last night I dreamed about a dancing French fry. Maybe that means something?

As for Emmet, I kind of wish you'd leave him alone. He never told me about finding a knife in the woods. He's not someone who would even <u>have</u> a knife. I think--well, I think maybe he's just too sensitive to survive in the real world--sort of like a poet. People like that need friends.

Doug
"Ever ready with spaghetti"
(That would be the Italian hamburger.)

Well, woo-hoo! The illustrious Dr. Milton herself, here in person! Sorry, Doc, but I forgot to roll out the red carpet. You can just chill downstairs while I get this chapter ready. It's too bad you fired Messenger Guy. I'd gotten used to him. He was a creep, but at least we had a routine worked out.

You kinda look like him, you know? Under the plastic surgery, I mean. You both have that same kind of snooty, pointed face. He called you Mama lately?

Meow!

And you can get out of the huddle you're in with my mother. She doesn't know anything, about anything. Too bad!

Look, Milton, as far as the "true nature" of my relationship with Emmet—take a pill and go to bed, okay? I'm tired of your stupid questions. If I wanted, I could claw your eyes out.

By the way—nice hair. Is it Sassy Red, by Celebritease? You really should have it done professionally.

My hair color is natural.

Teens Involved in Illicit Relationship?

by **CARL BRENNER**
Mid-State News staff writer

GANTON—As reported on Channel 4, the siblings, ages 14 and 16, who allegedly attacked Nicholas Slanger were possibly involved in an incestuous relationship with one another.

When queried, Police Chief Wilkinson repeated his insistence that the public not believe everything it hears, stating that, "Any case involving a celebrity, even one as elusive as Nicholas Slanger, attracts false and salacious rumors." The police, Wilkinson continued, "are only concerned with determining if a crime has been committed, and if so, solving it."

The teenagers' mother and Dr. Rita Milton of the Tomington Center have both refused comment.

"Please," said Halden Colfax, sitting in a booth at the Pig Pie, "I'm eating my supper here." Washing down a bite of eggplant Parmesan with a swig of iced tea, he added, "People will say anything to get themselves in front of a camera, even lies. Those kids might be crazy, but this sex stuff is pushing it. I saw them all the time, and they never looked like they were getting it on to me."

However, Buck Fallow, a student who rode the school bus with the teenagers in question, said, "Yeah, man. Like, everybody knew."

THE FATHER PROJECT

Chapter Eight

Closing the attic door behind her, leaving Emmet alone with his wound, N. saw Doug standing in the hallway, staring at the stream of clothes spilled down the runner—dress slacks, white shirt, underwear, and socks.

"Oh, there you are," he said, his eyes brightening as they met hers. "I couldn't find you guys." His cheeks dimpled. "Are you all right?"

"Yes," she said, trying not to show the confusion raging in her heart. Was she losing her human side entirely? She had almost taken Emmet's *life.*

Doug waited for her to continue. When she didn't, he pretended to study the framed photographs hanging on the wall. "Melody? I know she's your cousin and all, but she's kind of weird. She told me she was going outside to smoke. So when I mentioned that cigarettes aren't really, you know, *good* for you, she said, 'Not *that* kind of smoking, dodo.' She called me a *dodo*! So forget it."

He nodded toward a posed picture of Emmet and N., taken when they were little. "You get that done at Pronto Photo? I've got one just like it, only I'm in a sailor suit. I was like three years old or something." He snuck a look at N., quickly dropping his eyes. "I thought I'd come help you and Em with dinner, but you weren't there." He shrugged, studying his feet. "So, uh, where'd Emmet go?" She followed his gaze to the clothes.

"Oh, he, um, had to take a bath." N. bent to pick up his things.

"Bath?"

"He spilled something on him, some, um, gravy, and I, uh, I had to get some stuff in the attic." She tossed Emmet's clothes into his bedroom.

"Oh. Well, a bath, yes. I took one before I came." He smiled shyly, his blue eyes skittering across N.'s face. "Dad says a bath is a man's best friend." He shrugged again and looked at a photograph of Aunt Tam and Uncle Arnie with Melody. "Our attic is full of old junk."

"Yeah. Ours, too. But I couldn't find what I needed."

"Oh. That's a nice picture of your mom. I've got a big one of my mother in my bedroom." He looked at her, his face suddenly charged with apprehension. "We moved it from the living room when Dad started dating Fiona, so, you know, Fiona wouldn't feel bad if she came to visit." He ran his fingers through his short blond hair. "Do you believe in ghosts?"

N. shrugged. *Ghost* was such a human concept.

"I do. The night Mom died, I couldn't fall asleep for anything, but then I did. All of a sudden I woke up, and there she was, sitting at the foot of my bed. She seemed, I don't know, peaceful or calm or something, maybe even smiling a little bit, like everything was okay." He stuck his hands in his pockets. "She didn't say anything. I guess I fell asleep again, because the next thing I knew it was morning and she was gone." He cleared his throat. "I keep thinking she might come back."

N. pushed her hair behind her ears. People were always getting caught up in sentiment.

Doug leaned to brush a piece of lint off his pants. "Anyway, I've been worried she'll be upset if she discovers we've moved her picture. Before she died, she told Dad to find someone new, and not spend the rest of his life grieving, but . . ." He shrugged, his blue eyes clouding over. "What if she's lonely?" He stared at the wall. "He still keeps a picture of her in his wallet. I've got one, too."

"Maybe your mother likes Fiona," N. offered, trying to hide her impatience. "Maybe she wants them to get married."

Doug blew air out through his lips. "I hope so. Except, well, Fiona turned him down, so I guess it doesn't matter anymore."

"So he asked her?" The small wounds on N.'s back burned and prickled. Did Mr. Bracken get down on one knee to propose? Had he already bought a ring? Why did humans equate love with happiness? In the wild, animals knew nothing of love, yet thrived. Grieve over someone for the rest of your life? No way. Yet everyone assumed she missed her father.

An image of his hands, big and wide, flitted through her head. Hands meant for farming, not for—

She swallowed. Not for *what*?

"He asked her last night at the dance, around ten-fifteen. Some guy named Craig won the bet. One hundred and twenty-six dollars." Doug tried to smile. "I guess we'll be moving the picture back into the living room."

N. struggled for normal—*human* normal—forcing herself to face Doug. "Everyone says it'll take a while for her to say yes." She cleared her throat. "Isn't there another pool going on?"

Doug grinned. "Yeah, that's true." They both studied another picture of N. and Emmet when they were small, this time holding hands in front of a swing set, N. grinning boldly, Emmet, awkward and shy, looking at the ground.

"So how come you didn't tell me who your mother's boyfriend was?"

"St. Nick?" A tall, skinny guy. A father-replacer. But also a mother-distracter. "What's to know?"

"Are you kidding? He's *Nicholas Slanger!*"

N. blinked. "Who?"

"The writer. Nicholas Slanger. You didn't know?"

Hair prickled up the back of N.'s neck. "I've never seen him before. And nobody mentioned his last name." Slanger was the guy who'd written that letter to Emmet! Something suggesting danger seemed to flit past her down the hallway. A ghost?

"You might end up famous, if your Mom marries him."

"Are you sure that's who it is?" *He knew about wings.*

"I saw him once at the Pig Pie. And then he gave me that letter for Em. When I came in today, I didn't realize it was him, because I didn't look. I made straight for you. And for Emmet, I mean." N., her jaw tightening, watched his face flame. "I didn't know he was sitting on the couch."

N. moved mechanically toward the stairs, then stopped, dread weighting her legs. "You're *certain*?"

Doug shrugged. "Unless this guy is an impersonator. I mean, it's strange, because I didn't think he hardly ever left his house, much less dated anyone." He rocked back on his heels. "And he's as weird as everybody says he is. Before I came searching for you guys, he came over to the drinks table. I told him I'd given you Emmet's letter, but he just gave me a wink. When I turned to leave, he said, 'Be forewarned, boy—the cat is out, the hunt is on!'"

N. froze. "He said *what*?"

"That a cat—"

A soft yowl escaped N.'s throat. Only Doug's anxious hand clasped on her arm kept her human.

Doug carried a tray of cheese and crackers around the room, and N. manned the drinks table. Trying to keep her hands from shaking, she poured wine for Aunt Tam. "Thank you, dear," her aunt said, smiling generously. N. didn't respond, carefully setting down the bottle.

"I know it can't be easy meeting your mother's new friend," Aunt Tam continued. "And a famous writer, at that! Did she tell you how they met? She got a flat tire out past the Pig Pie; he was driving by and stopped to change it for her. He's really quite charming. Not at all odd, like everybody thinks. But that's the press for you." She sipped her wine. "I know you're interested in fantasy, and now you have the master himself to talk to. You could even show him one of your own stories. Do you know how many people would kill for that opportunity? What a lucky girl you are!" She walked back across the room.

N. stole a look at Slanger.

Sitting on the couch, his arm around her mother's shoulders, he tilted his head to return her stare, a small, sly smile on his face.

N. dropped her eyes. First he'd known about wings, then he'd mentioned a cat. How could he know those things? And why was he dating her mother? A cold shiver danced up and down her spine. Oh, for fur to warm her! She picked up the bottle of Coke, but there was no one to pour it for. Slightly dizzy, she set it back down.

Doug, still standing across the room holding the plate of cheese and crackers, talked to Uncle Arnie.

A small noise turned her head. Emmet stood next to her, his body tight with uncertainty, his mouth a thin line of tension, anxiety swimming in his eyes—a small but angry red slash above his eye, under his eyebrow. Why hadn't he told her about Slanger? But maybe he hadn't realized; he'd probably only ever seen him from above. Or maybe he *had* recognized him—and was simply too frightened to say.

An odd warmth flooded N.'s heart—her still-human need to protect and nurture. "Come with me," she said, leading the way to the downstairs bathroom. He followed her like a small child.

She closed the toilet seat and parked him on top, then opened the medicine cabinet. What was good for eyelids?

"Gosh, what happened?" Doug asked, sticking his head around the open door.

Emmet jerked at his voice, wincing, but N. pulled his chin back, daring to touch, feeling him tremble. "He slipped getting out of the tub. He's all right." She dampened a ball of cotton with antiseptic, and dabbed his eyelid.

"Really? Too bad. Does it hurt?"

Emmet didn't answer, not able to speak. N. met his eyes, their deep, feral depth approaching frenzy. As much as she longed for total transformation, Emmet needed it more. He always had. He wouldn't be able to tolerate his human side much longer.

"It only hurts a little," she answered for him.

"I think your mother's still pissed that you took the roast out early. I'm glad she liked my cheese and crackers idea, though. There's nothing like a snack before dinner, Dad always says." He watched N. work on Emmet. "By the way, did you like my poem?"

N. narrowed her eyes. "Poem?"

"You know. About Dad and Fiona." He beamed at Emmet. "You can read it, too, if you like. It's not finished yet, but I think it's pretty good. It's for the Father Project."

Emmet blinked.

"Oh," N. said. "Your poem. Yeah, it was great. I liked it." The Father Project was *such* a stupid idea.

"So," Doug said, "what do you want to know about the clearing in the woods?"

N. blinked.

"Isn't that one of the reasons you invited me?"

Emmet followed N. into the narrow hallway, standing beside her like a puppy too frightened to move. The three of them crowded together in front of the bathroom door, careful not to touch.

N. smoothed her velvety blue dress down over her hips. Sensing Doug's eyes following her hands, she stopped, her face growing hot. Why did she react to being looked at? How stupidly human. Just because he was such a *boy*, that didn't mean she had to be such a *girl*. She crossed her arms over her chest. "Who made the clearing? Slanger?"

Doug frowned. "I don't know. I think it's just *there*, and has been for a long time. It doesn't look new. Maybe it's where the Indians had a teepee or something."

N. sniffed. *Right*. Pocahontas, herself. "Can you get there from here, through the woods?"

"Sure," he said. "All the paths cross at one point or another. I've followed most of them, even as far as Slanger's place. Not that I've ever stopped by and said hi or anything."

N. looked at Emmet. Should she tell him about Slanger's letter?

"I come here through the woods all the time," Doug continued. "I see you in your yard a lot." He twisted his mouth in dismay at N.'s startled response. "I mean—" His face turned red all over again. "Not that I—I mean—I'm not spying or anything." He looked frantically at

Emmet. "I'm just out exploring and stuff. I'm not doing anything weird."

Emmet's eyes bore into Doug's, confused, as if, in the course of one afternoon, he no longer understood human embarrassment, or even a boy's desire to look at a girl. Unfortunately, N. did. For a moment, she didn't know if her racing pulse had more to do with the possibility of Doug seeing her in her cat shape, or in her girl shape. Especially her changing-back, girl-without-clothes-on-yet shape.

She cleared her throat. "Does Slanger ever go to the clearing?"

"I don't know. I've never seen him there. Just the occasional deer, and sometimes a fox. Once I saw a—"

A pleasant voice interrupted. "Are you kids finished with the bathroom?"

Startled, N. turned to find Nicholas Slanger leaning nonchalantly against the wall. "I need to use the facilities," he explained, smiling. He smelled like the woods.

N. automatically stepped aside, leaving Emmet still blocking the door.

"Well?" He looked kindly at Emmet, who stood frozen in place. "The sky is yours, Emmet," he said, softly. "Beware, though. Grand on the wing, you're still no more than flesh-and-bone on the ground."

"Excuse me?" Doug stood with his arms crossed. "No offense, but we don't speak *Fantasy* here."

Slanger chuckled, his eyes bright. "We'll understand each other soon enough. Even you, little bunny."

N. snarled, but Slanger merely raised his eyebrows at her. "We share a common interest in the woods, don't we, dear? And in your brother. But there's no need to worry, he's in no danger from me." He turned to Emmet, smiling sweetly. "And now, young man, I really must take a leak."

Doug grabbed Emmet's arm and pulled him aside. "All right," he said hotly. "We get *that* message. You know, for a famous person, you're really kind of rude!"

"Indeed?" Slanger laughed, stepping into the bathroom. He turned just before he shut the door in Doug's face. "Run, little children! Run!"

They fled.

Tearing out the back door, they crashed into Melody, landing in a heap on the ground. Clawing his way out of the sprawl, Emmet scrambled for the woods, barely making it to the first straggly tree before he transformed, soaring into the sky.

Only N., jumping to her feet and running after him, witnessed his change. She tossed his clothes behind a bush as Doug tried to disentangle himself from Melody, who, giggling hysterically, wrapped her long arms and legs around him repeatedly. Finally he stood up, free, his face scarlet.

N. walked back toward the house, her lips twisted into a sick grin, fear grinding her gut. "Emmet went for a walk," she said. Doug's nose twitched uncertainly as he looked toward the woods.

Emmet Marcona
Tomington Center—Wing A—Dr. Milton
Assignment
November 15

I don't know why I'm writing again on the same day.
Something feels urgent, though. I don't know what.
Can I use the phone and call Niki? I can talk, you
know; I just haven't.

I know it sounds crazy, but I don't think this isolation
is good for me. All I've ever wanted is to be alone,
but before, my aloneness was surrounded by others.
Niki was always there for me, <u>always</u>, even when I
wanted her to go away. Even if she exacted a
price.

And Doug was just down the road, or on the bus.
Every time I thought to use my computer, there was
an e-mail from him. And Mom was in the background.
I don't know if she ever really loved me, but she was
there. Now I'm surrounded by—nothing. No one.
Silence.

I find myself listening for the aides. Listening for
your footsteps coming down the hall. Does that
make me pathetic?

I wish I could go away. I could, if you'd let me. If you
stopped giving me this medication. It holds me down
or something, a captive.

Listen, sometimes I slip so fast, the air turning so rapidly, that the in-between moment is barely there. Like the day of the dinner party, when I was tearing out the back door with Niki and Doug. It was crazy kid stuff—Mom was mad at us for taking the roast out too early, and we ran squealing out the door as if we were five-year-olds, stumbling into Melody, falling, jumping up, running again toward the woods—

I projected immediately into otherness, lost in air that thickened all about me. I could see clearly. All around me, space extended forever, as if I were up in the sky. Not separate from it at all, but of it, a part of it. Wildness was upon me, and I wasn't frightened, not one bit. I was immensely happy! Free, alone in my solitude, embraced by the wind, knowing it would last forever.

It didn't. It never does. The disturbance—the change in the air—smoothes itself out. The unavoidable hiccup, of time or space, is gone. It always makes me sad when it ends, but it always ends. I find myself alone in the woods, dazed and chilled.

Don't you think this kind of thing happens to everyone, though, in some form or other? It doesn't mean I'm insane. Reality becomes difficult, so you seek escape. Music, art, drugs—even fantasies, like the ones Niki writes. I've read that art is the way we shape the random events of life, and give it meaning. Even Slanger must need to explain things.

What about you, Dr. Milton?

That Sunday, when I finally turned to go home, a long black snake slithered right under my foot. Now, <u>that</u> frightened me!

I know black snakes are harmless, though—at least to people—so I calmed myself and continued on. Stepping into my yard, I caught a flash of something red just at the edge of the wood. A fox?

For a moment, I stood frozen, remembering the dream I told you about—a fox that disappeared, leaving in its stead a beautiful woman wrapped in a mossy green cloak, her hair tangled and wild and red. She laughed and released a bird from her wrist. In my dream, I watched it go.

Maybe I dream when I'm both awake and asleep. I've heard that schizophrenia is something like that—a dream while you're awake. Is that what you think is wrong with me? Then how can I think so clearly? As I write, each word follows logic, not madness.

Like the bird in my dream that struggled its way to the sky, maybe I'm simply lost from someone's gauntlet, adrift.

From: Douglas Bracken <dougman@minimen.com>
To: Dr. Rita I. Milton <Milton@tellet.com>
Sent: Saturday, November 16—5:43 AM
Subject: Re: Emmet's Knife

Dr. Milton,

I'm in kind of a rush here--I work the breakfast shift at the Pig Pie today. It might be that washing dishes is something I can put on my resume later in life, as real-life experience. It might make me seem more handsome or something. I think writers do stuff like that a lot.

If Emmet told you about a knife, but nobody could find it, not even in his room, then maybe there never was a knife? He could have imagined it, though that's more like something Niki would do. I've never seen either of them get violent--I mean, except for Halloween night. Well, this one time Niki almost hit me, but it was an accident. I walked up behind her at school and touched her on the arm. I was just trying to get her attention, but I guess I startled her pretty badly. She had this kind of crazy look in her eye--but this was right after her father disappeared, so I guess she was on edge. She was OK in a minute.

To answer your question, I only saw Mr. Slanger the one time, when he came into the Pig Pie. Why do you suppose writers are so mysterious? Strange childhoods?

Doug Bracken
"Washer of kitchen knives and forks,
    Always clean, never a dork."

Why did you ask me about my mother? You've been talking to her downstairs for half an hour. Again. Can't you figure her out on your own? It's pretty simple, really. Her husband dumped her and she's raising two kids alone. Hello? You need a degree for that?

I think you're a little too involved with the Marconas right now. Don't you have other patients, or do they only let you do one family group at a time?

There's always baby-boy Weasel. He could take up some of your time. He's got this kind of murderous look about him that you might want to check out. A few years in the slammer should help.

Listen. Mom's basically a good person, so I try to be nice to her. Sure, she's gone out on a few dates here and there—who wants to look like a total loser? But it's nothing serious.

It's true that I can do some things that she can't. Not all talents are shared. So, no—she can't transform.

Can you?

Mother Threatens Lawsuit

by CARL BRENNER
Mid-State News staff writer

GANTON—The mother of the two teenagers accused of allegedly attacking Nicholas Slanger in the woods on Halloween night has stated, through her lawyer, that she is considering legal action against *Mid-State News* and Channel 4, which are owned by the same company.

"My children have committed none of the reprehensible actions freely referred to over and over again by *Mid-State News* and Channel 4 television. Without facts to back up accusations, rumors become libel and slander."

It is widely known in the area that the woman's son is being treated at the Tomington Center, while her daughter is receiving treatment at home.

Tomington Center refused comment, as did Chief Wilkinson. Legal experts feel the mother does not have a case. But Brian Angsbee, a local resident, agreed with the mother. Taking time out from his French fries and barbecued chicken at the Pig Pie, he said, "The media has just been piling it on. What have these kids really done? Nothing. What crime has actually been committed? None! What we've got here is imagination run wild."

Fiona Tony, a hostess at the Pig Pie, said, "I've kept silent so far, but I'm with Brian. Enough already. The media needs to go away and leave those kids alone."

Tony is engaged to the father of the boy who first alerted the police on Halloween night.

THE FATHER PROJECT

Chapter Nine

Buck Fallow pursed his lips and smacked them obscenely at N. as he passed her, heading for the back of the bus. Scrunching down in her seat, she slunk closer to Emmet's arm.

Since coming back to school on the Monday following Emmet's "biting" incident, they had been ridiculed mercilessly. Three days of jeers and whispers about *Beak Boy*, and digs about *Hiss*, had left her nerves jangled. Just that morning, Debba Watson had bumped into N. as she leaned over a water fountain. "Meo-o-w!" Debba had shrieked, right in N.'s ear, startling her and sending her tumbling to the floor. *Yeo-o-w!* As Debba curled her lip in a cruel laugh, N.'s nails sprang open, unsheathed, and she had to forcibly conceal them. Oh, for one swipe at her face!

Now it was Samatha Kaylo's turn to insult, hopping down the center of the bus, flapping her arms and chirping. N. wanted to leap onto her back and dig with her claws; instead, she burrowed into Emmet's arm.

He tensed at her touch but allowed it. Staring resolutely out the window at the sky, he was barely there. He'd survived the jeers and taunts because he'd hardly noticed them. Since Sunday's dinner with Slanger, he seemed to be locked even deeper in his hawk's mind.

The bus finally started its run to take them home. Safe for the moment, N. drifted into a quick, delicious sleep. A lurch, though, dislodged her, and she felt a crunch in her pocket—the e-mail from Doug she'd printed out that morning, folded up and forgotten. He'd been home sick for three days with a ferocious cold—his Sunday sneeze had proven fateful.

Ordinarily, she wouldn't have noticed his absence, much—but

things weren't ordinary anymore. She was keenly aware that, for three days, he hadn't sat in his protective position in the seat behind them. Besides, he seemed intent on not letting her forget about him. Every time she went to the computer—there he was.

She unfolded the piece of paper.

Hi! Hope those idiots aren't still bothering u and Em. They're creeps and turds. If I was sitting behind u on the bus, I'd give every one of them a big fat lip. :)

She couldn't imagine Doug giving anyone anything even remotely resembling a big fat lip.

My fever finally went down, so I guess I'm not dying ... (yay! lol) ... Fiona came over on her break last night and made me hot tea with lemon and sugar!!!! mmmmmmm. Dad wasn't even home. She says she loves him, but she's not sure she's ready for marriage. Dad thinks the tea is a good sign, though ... He says that when a woman makes u a cup of anything, it's evidence of domesticity. He's invited her to go to the movies. Swordo's Sheath is playing at the B-Grade. They're running a special: if u buy the He-Man popcorn, u get two free small sodas ... she's thinking about it.

I added more verses to my poem.

> Dad took Fiona on a date--
> They had lasagna. They went on a second date, then
>   another.
> Sometimes, though, she made him wait,
> Which made it hard to think she might turn into his wife, or
>   my mother.

(Though at fifteen, of course, I don't need one. I'm self-
   sufficient. Fate
Didn't give me a sister or brother.)

Do you think that last part is too philosophical? Maybe I don't
need the parentheses.

Would they get married? The Pig Pie
Took bets, offering onion-fried steak,
Half-price, to anyone putting down money--though I,
As a minor, couldn't participake.
It'd be great if they did marry, I thought, and ate some
   fries--
After all, men who are old and fat need a break.

Should I drop the part about Dad being fat? I don't want to hurt his
feelings ... but he is ... kinda ... I'm hoping it's not hereditary.

One night they went dancing, country.
Dad wore his string tie and Western shirt.
"Fiona," he said, "you're my sweetie.
Marry me, please, or my life is dirt."
It was 10:15. She said, "No." Dad said, "Phooey."
Some guy named Craig won the bet. This would rhyme if his
   name had been Bert.

That's all so far ... I hope Fiona changes her mind and says yes, so
I can give my poem a happy ending. The deadline for the Father
Project is coming up, though, so there isn't much time left ... did
you decide 2 write something? Maybe u should ... definitely makes
you think. Hey, next week's Halloween! What ru guys doing? I
guess I'll be back in school soon.
c ya--Doug.

The bus screeched to a halt opposite their house, and N. climbed off, followed by Emmet. As they crossed the street, she could sense him already transforming in his mind, shedding his clothes, climbing the air—his body a tightly bound wire, ready to spring.

What if he didn't come back?

N. swallowed hard. Her nature was different from his. She could see herself sometime in the future, totally transformed—yet still close, even showing up to worm her way into her mother's affection, wrapping herself around her ankles, being petted on the head. But Emmet? He'd be gone.

And if he came back, she'd be his prey.

She stopped in front of their yard—the driveway empty, their mother not yet home—and watched him head to the door to dump his backpack. How long before he was lost to her forever? Before danger overruled love? A darkness filled her heart. And fear.

She heard a car barreling down the road, slowing as it approached their house. Emmet turned to look, and so did she, stepping quickly aside as a car pulled off the road. She waited, uncertain. Who was it? A man stepped out.

Slanger!

He walked swiftly around the car, approaching her, a smile on his face. Hair stood up on N.'s neck and she tensed, prepared to—

"So Doug Bracken gave Emmet's letter to *you*. I thought he might." A light gleamed in his eyes. "Boys will be boys, now, won't they." He stepped closer, his eyes piercing, hypnotic, his hand reaching, slowly, to touch—and N. jumped back, fear constricting her into a tight, cold muscle. She heard Emmet cross the yard, coming up behind her, his footsteps crunching the leaves—some remembrance of being a brother.

Slanger dropped his hand. "Emmet, I hoped you'd be home. How nice to see you again." He chuckled, glancing at the woods, then back. "I was just telling your sister how glad I am she's friends with Doug. Everyone should have a confidant." His eyes didn't seem to blink. "You, especially, should have a friend. Why don't you meet me behind the Bracken place next Thursday night, and we can talk." He laughed. "That's Halloween, by the way. I hope you'll forgive my sense of humor." He suddenly flapped his arms. "Gawk! Gawk!"

The blood that had drained to N.'s feet charged back to her heart. "Bastard!" she shrieked, unleashing her claws, swiping—

He smacked her arm aside, his movements a confusing blur. N. blinked stupidly as pinpoints of pain pricked her skin. "*Sorry, sweetie,*" he said. "Guess I don't know my own strength. But don't worry, I won't tell your mother about our little altercation—she probably wouldn't be pleased to know you tried to hit me." He lifted his eyebrows, then turned on his heel, striding back to his car. In a moment, he was gone.

N. pushed up her sleeve, staring at two tiny spots of blood on her arm. What had he done? It had happened so fast—she gulped, frightened and drained of energy. She needed to curl up, sleep, forget this. Forget everything. She needed a lap. Soft fur sprang up on her skin.

Emmet, bewildered, reached tentatively, pointing at her arm. "Cut?" he asked.

N. shook her head no.

"Then—what?" Emmet struggled for understanding.

It looked like a small bite. "Nothing. I don't know what it is." She squeezed her eyes shut. What did this mean?

She opened her eyes. "Last week, Slanger handed Doug a letter to give to you. Doug gave it to me, instead." She looked at Emmet's face, grown pale and wan, his brown eyes unhappy. "You were so upset, I didn't want you to read it. It's about Dad. And wings." She cleared her throat. "Slanger said—"

"Hey!" Doug trotted toward them from the side of the house, and N. quickly pulled down her sleeve. "What was Mr. Slanger doing here? I saw him drive off." He grinned. "I was feeling better, so I thought I'd go for a walk. Then, what the heck, I decided to cut through the woods to your house—you know, since we talked about it and all. I thought you guys might be getting home about now." He looked from N.'s face to Emmet's, his smile fading. "What's wrong?"

Emmet opened his mouth, then shut it. He tried again. "Letter?"

"Huh?" Doug scrunched up his nose.

"The letter you gave me," said N., "from Slanger. I, um, never gave it to Emmet. I read it myself."

"Oh." Doug studied the leaves around his feet, then looked up. "Yeah. I read it, too."

"You *did?*" Shock smacked N. in the face. He'd read it? How dare he!

Doug squared his jaw, belligerent. "Well, it wasn't sealed. And it was from a *famous author*. Who gets that kind of mail?" He shrugged. "So I peeked." He frowned at N. "I'm not as stupid as you think I am. It doesn't take a genius IQ to figure out that Emmet's got some kind of weirdo bird thing going. Slanger's probably interested because he wants to write a spooky story with a bird in it or something."

N. sensed Emmet's body tensing tighter and tighter next to hers— ready to explode into the air.

Doug's eyes traveled defiantly down N.'s human body, then back up to her face. "And *you*—you pretend you're a cat half the time. It's not like it isn't obvious." His nose twitched indignantly as N. opened her mouth, astonished. "Don't act like it isn't true. I mean, it's probably just psychological or something, because of your father."

He stood taller and straightened his shoulders. "I know what it's like to lose a parent. Stuff happens. I figured you guys needed a friend." He looked at Emmet. "Slanger is probably just being nosy. I mean, it's got to be a pretty good deal for a fantasy writer, to discover that your girlfriend's got two kids who think they're animals." He turned to N. "You still got the letter?"

She nodded.

"Let's go look at it, then. No point in Emmet being freaked." He led the way to N.'s front door. Numbly, they followed.

Emmet Marcona
Tomington Center—Wing A—Dr. Milton
Assignment
November 17

Nicholas Slanger? I've already told you about him.

When I'd walk in the woods near his place, sometimes
I'd see him standing in the trees, just watching. He
never said anything. Never called my name or
lifted his hand in greeting. I don't like being
watched.

Then, one day he spoke to me. I hardly knew what
he was saying, I was so scared. He taunted me, as if
he knew there was something I wanted, but was too
frightened to pursue. As if he knew what it was.
Daring me. We met this way for weeks; I grew hungry
for his words. Then he handed me a knife. Why
would he do such a thing? I threw it on the ground
and fled.

One day, Niki told me about a letter from him that
she'd kept hidden from me. My chest felt funny, like
something was trapped inside, trying to get out. Why
would he write me a letter? Did he want his knife
back? But I threw it on the ground, I'm sure I did. He
could have just picked it up.

To be honest, for a moment, I hoped the letter

wasn't from him at all, but from Dad. Impossible, I know. Dad didn't much like me when he was here—why would he write?

I used to watch the mail, but that was a long time ago, before I understood the finality of good-bye, before I knew that emptiness could last forever. Now I don't even think about mail. Or phone calls. Dad left us. He's gone.

You know what? That funny feeling is in my chest right now—a fluttering, as if a bird were trapped inside. As if I were dying.

I know you want me to cooperate. I _am_ cooperating. But I need to be let out, set free. You'd let a trapped bird go, wouldn't you?

But maybe you're a hunter, just like Niki. I'm not blind, I see you watching me every day, observing me as if I were a wild animal, trying to find and capture my soul. You never will, but I understand that it's your nature to try.

I wish that in-between moment would come, right now, and I could slip away. I'd like to be in that thickness again, in that different place. But right now I'm just Emmet, writing this assignment. For you, Dr. Milton.

From: Douglas Bracken <dougman@minimen.com>
To: Dr. Rita I. Milton <Milton@tellet.com>
Sent: Wednesday, November 20—4:53 PM
Subject: Re: The Neighborhood

Dr. Milton,

Yes, now that you mention it, I guess everybody around these woods is a little strange. Well, not Dad. Except for his dismissal of the vegetable family, he's pretty normal. Although--did I tell you this?--I fixed cauliflower (steamed) with cheese sauce (Cheez Whiz) and he ate it. So there's hope.

I guess Nicholas Slanger would count as odd, considering all the weird stuff everyone is saying about him, and for sure he lives (lived?) in the woods. Plus he was your patient, right? I recently saw something on TV about Alzheimer's. Has anyone considered that might be why he's missing? He is kind of old. People with dementia sometimes wander off and get lost. He could have gotten run over by a truck or something.

One thing I've wondered about is why nobody knows who Mr. Marcona's mistress is, since that's who he ran away with. Dad says that most mistresses these days are proud to be cheats and don't mind having their picture in the paper or on TV, so you'd think there would be some information by now. It might take some steam out of the HE'S MISSING, TOO, rumor mill. (That's what Dad thinks the Mid-State News is. A rumor mill. He likes the Frontier, the paper Mr. Marcona wrote for, but he thinks Mid-State is a liberal rag. Did I mention that Dad's a Republican? And Fiona's a Democrat? I'm a little worried about that. What will happen during election years?)

Your question about Niki and Emmet kind of creeped me out. Dr.

Milton, nothing porno was going on between them. That's gross, and <u>not true.</u>

Bottom line: Emmet wouldn't let anyone touch him.

But I know you believe Niki and Emmet are sick. You think they got weird in the woods and I was so freaked I ran and hit my head on a tree and passed out, then called the cops. I <u>did</u> run and bang my head, but not because of sex stuff. Because of spooky dark-night stuff. It didn't help that it was Halloween.

Listen, Dr. Milton. Sometimes when you're depressed, sadness just takes over your life. After my mother died, I was a hedgehog for months. I told you that already. But that doesn't mean I turned into a <u>sicko</u>. If you've ever been really sad and lonely, you'd understand. Well, I guess you were lonely and sad when your son died.

Dr. Milton, since you know how hard it can be sometimes to just <u>breathe</u>, couldn't you cut Em and Niki some slack? I think they're pretending to be animals just so they can take a break from being so stressed and <u>human</u> all the time. So maybe you could give them some Prozac or something, but let Emmet come home and Niki go back to school? (?) I miss them.

I think if they came back, and were allowed to be <u>normal</u> again, all this crazy talk--along with the reporters and cops--would go away.

Doug
"Once curled up in a ball
 Happy about nothing at all"

P.S. I was wondering--are you related to John Milton, the great poet? I haven't exactly read the whole thing (it's <u>really</u> long) but he wrote this huge poem about losing paradise. I kind of feel like that's what's happening now, to Niki and Em. And to the woods.

Why are you talking to my mother again?
You need a friend, is that it? Nobody loves
you? Aw-w-w-w.

I know—why don't you adopt Weasel-
face? Since he looks like you. Be a mommy!
In the meantime, leave my mother alone. At
least Emmet and I don't need to resort to
plastic surgery to look human. Or animal.
We can switch back and forth as we need to.
We can—

Dang golly gee, what an interesting
thought I've just had. In some kind of low-
rent transformation, a weasel-boy tries to
look more human, a human boy more like a
weasel. A famous psychiatrist hires him to
scare the local loonies, and a movie plot is
born! Look out, Oscar!

So—who wins best actor?
Weasel-boy? Or you?

Teen Confesses?

by **CARL BRENNER**
Mid-State News staff writer

GANTON—This reporter has learned, through an unnamed source, that the teenage girl allegedly involved in the disappearance of Nicholas Slanger on Halloween night has given a written account of the events leading up to that night to Dr. Rita I. Milton. Dr. Milton is treating the girl's brother at the Tomington Center for Psychiatric Disorders.

The source, who claims to have read the girl's account, says that, while fanciful, it is provocative in the extreme, and may hold clues to what actually happened.

Both Dr. Milton and the Tomington Center have declined comment.

However, Chief Wilkinson said, "If true, we'd like to see it. We'll obtain a court order, if necessary."

Dr. Milton has been seen entering and leaving the girl's residence, and was once spotted by this reporter getting into her car near the entrance to the drive that leads to Slanger's house. Slanger's property has become a lure for some of his fans who hope to catch a glimpse of their hero and prove, at least to themselves, that he's not missing.

"Truth is stranger than fiction, man," said Dale Emberly, 16 years old, while eating an apple fritter at the Pig Pie. "If she wrote it, let's read it."

Many people in the Ganton area apparently share his opinion.

THE FATHER PROJECT

Chapter Ten

Sitting at the kitchen table with her brother and Doug, N. toyed with the ceramic hound-dog salt- and pepper shakers guarding the napkin holder. Her mother had bought them at the county fair last summer, along with a pound of fudge.

She and Emmet had appeared to be the only teenagers dorky enough to show up at the fair with a parent. In August's sweltering heat, it had been pleasantly difficult to separate human smell from animal. Still, N. knew that the crowds, both human and animal, had frightened Emmet—except in the small animal barn, where, among the chickens and rabbits, he seemed to lose fear and gain a ferocious longing. N. herself would have liked to slink away, scoot around at the edges of everything, and hunt the mice that darted through the shadows.

Only in the buildings sheltering the prize-winning cabbages and giant zucchinis, the homemade cakes and pies, did they feel steadily human—they could wander more or less as people, smelling like people, and, in the crafts section, buy stuff.

She set the hound dogs down and watched as Emmet read the letter from Slanger, his hands trembling slightly as his eyes worked their way worriedly down the page, his mouth a tight slash.

Doug, elbows on the table, popped air out through his lips—which sounded a whole lot like a fart. He looked at N. and smiled. People chose the most foolish moments to be happy. Did he understand that she and Emmet were as much animal as human?

N. gave him a small smile back. No, he didn't know. He knew normal things, like e-mail and *More Tits Video*, and the noise manufactured by Dram Skeetch.

Emmet finally spoke, his voice frightened. "He wants to talk to me. About Dad." N. watched a strange emotion flit across his face. Did he even remember their father—*really* remember him? She recalled a simple gesture—her father's hand lightly touching Emmet's head as he sat at this very kitchen table eating a bowl of cereal, hunched over a graphic novel, *Ravenay #6, Total Destruction*. How long ago was that? Forever ago.

"How did Slanger find out about—the flying?" Emmet had trouble getting the words out.

Doug shrugged, lifting his arm to wipe his nose on his sleeve, stopping just in time. He grabbed a napkin out of the napkin holder. "That you're into birds? Probably from your mom. I mean, it's kind of obvious. Everybody knows you're a little bit crazy." He laughed. "Well, not *crazy*. It's just—like when we're on the bus? You're always looking out the window and staring up at the sky. If you see a bird, even just a dinky sparrow, you turn into Bird Man or something. You even tilt your head to look at it with each eye, as if they weren't both on the front of your face. And you make some kind of chirring noise. Sometimes I think I can almost see feathers sprout."

He stuffed the napkin into his pocket. "I'm not the only one who's noticed." He turned to N. "And you're always acting either slinky or snarly. I've heard you hiss and stuff. Word gets around." He studied his hands, then smiled at her lightly.

Snarly? N. glared back at him. She was not snarly! And he was wrong about their mother. She didn't know anything. So maybe Doug yakked their business at the Pig Pie, and Slanger overheard people talking when he picked up a carryout. "Did *you* tell Slanger about us?"

Doug thrust his jaw forward. "Of course not!"

N. pushed her hair behind her ears. "Okay, okay. But why did he give the letter to *you*?"

Doug picked up the hound-dog saltshaker, pretending to study it. "He probably didn't want to approach you directly, since you didn't know about him and your mom yet. I mean, you two would be a pretty good subject for him. Your mom might not have liked that." He picked up the pepper dog, balancing it on his palm, then placed it nose-to-nose on the table with the salt. "Did you get these at the county fair last summer? I liked the skunks, but Dad wanted the porcupines, so that's what we ended up with."

N. glanced out the window, her nose twitching. They'd bought the *porcupine* shakers?

Wait—what was that? A movement out the window caught N.'s eye. That black cat again. She leaned and watched as it crouched on the lawn, staring up at her through the window. Odd. She tapped on the glass. The cat didn't move. She tapped louder, making Emmet squinch his brows and look at her in irritation. Doug half rose and leaned over her shoulder, and together they watched the cat study them, then whip its head toward the woods. Crouching low, stalking slowly, it suddenly broke form and streaked across the lawn, disappearing into the underbrush.

"That must be the cat your mom was talking about," Doug said. "I wonder what it's chasing. It's kind of rough-looking, don't you think?" He sat back down. "I guess it has to be, to survive in the wild. Whiskers was really gentle. I'd like to get another cat, but Dad says—"

"So Slanger just came up to you?" N. turned from the window.

He blew air out through his lips again. "Pretty much. He sat in his car and waved an envelope at me. 'Would you do me a favor and give this to Emmet Marcona?' I was like, '*Huh?*' because he's so famous and everything. My mouth was hanging open somewhere down around my ankles. So he said, 'A letter,' and stuffed it in my hands and started to pull away. Then he stopped and laughed, saying, 'And keep an eye out for that sister of his. She looks like trouble!'"

Doug's lips parted in a sheepish grin. "He must have thought I liked you or something."

N.'s tail twitched—or would have, if it had been present. So she was *trouble*?

"I'm home!" Her mother's voice sailed into the kitchen from the living room, her footsteps following, clicking their way down the hall.

N. jumped up and grabbed a bag of Oreos off the counter, throwing them on the table. "Act normal!" she hissed. "Eat!" She grabbed Slanger's letter out of Emmet's hands and jammed it into her pocket.

Doug tore the bag open and rammed three cookies into his mouth; Emmet took one and held it to his lips, then set it down, as if he couldn't figure out its purpose. N. chomped one in half and chewed.

"Oh, there you are," Mrs. Marcona said pleasantly, as she entered the kitchen, flipping through the pile of mail she carried. "Hi, Doug! I see you guys found the cookies. Honey, why don't you offer Doug a glass of milk?" She continued going through envelopes as N. got up from the table. N. tried not to notice Doug struggling with his mouthload of cookies, crumbs cascading down his chin. Milk was probably a good idea.

"I'm really glad you finally met Nick. He's a lovely man, not the way people say he is at all. He really wants to be friends with you." She laughed ruefully. "I invited him to Aunt Tam's Halloween party, but he's busy that night. My first party in two years, and my date can't come. Oh, well." She dumped the mail on the counter. "If you guys are interested, though, let me know. You're always welcome." She rubbed her face. "What a day! Don't ever teach fifth graders. They'll absolutely kill you."

N. waited till her mother's footsteps had faded down the hall. Did her mother have no clue that Slanger was a creep?

"He said he wants to meet me Halloween night," Emmet whispered, looking from Doug to N. with stricken eyes. "At nine o'clock—when it's dark."

"Spooky," agreed Doug, fishing for another Oreo.

"Emmet doesn't like being out at night," N. explained, shaking her head at the cookie Doug offered her.

"I'll go with you," he said, cheerfully. "It'll be fun. We can all go. See what kind of costume famous authors wear on Halloween." He pulled an Oreo in half and scraped the icing off with his teeth. "We'll have to bring flashlights."

N. remembered her mother's suggestion about milk and went to the refrigerator. Take Doug along? Someone fully human? She returned to the table, thrusting the filled glass toward Doug, just as he picked up the hound-dog pepper shaker. *Crack!* Their hands collided in midair, both of them jumping back as glass shattered, sending a torrent of milk all over the hound dog and the table, launching tiny slivers of glass into their hands.

They charged to the sink. N. picked a sliver out of Doug's palm, blood from a cut on her finger leaking into his wound. He held her finger up to the light and flicked away a thin, bright shard.

"Wow," he said. "Now we're blood brothers." He ran his hand under the faucet as N. splashed her finger through the stream of water. "We'll have to defend each other against all evil foes, like Lancelot and King Arthur. Before Guinevere showed up." He studied his palm.

N. turned off the water and tore sheets of paper towel, turning to find Emmet holding out a bottle of antiseptic and a box of Band-Aids. She watched Doug blot his wound. Maybe it would be good to have him along. Someone well versed in humanspeak, with no threat of transformation.

No hint of wing or claw.

Emmet Marcona
Tomington Center—Wing A—Dr. Milton
Assignment
November 22

What was in his letter? Everything.

Slanger said he knew about the meanness of
fathers. And that he understood how it is for a boy
who needs to spread his wings.

How could he have known? Somehow, he did.

I didn't tell anyone—I haven't even told you, before
now—but from that moment I began to think he
might be my friend. I wanted to talk to him, find
out how he knew that when I took one step into the
woods, and then another, I didn't ever want to
leave. How, when the in-between moment came—
however it came—and a thickness surrounded me,
all I could imagine was change—taking the air, and
moving through it with a swiftness that astounded.
How I couldn't even imagine walking in my same body
anymore.

I wanted to ask how he knew about my father, how
he knew about me.

So maybe you're right, Dr. Milton. Perhaps it's not a
turning in the air, after all, that causes those

in-between moments. Perhaps I am the one turning, and the slipping away is entirely my own doing, my own choice.

Was Slanger telling me to slip away for good, so I could become the true self I couldn't otherwise be? That it was finally time to leave?

I thought that if I talked to him—just him and me— that might be what he'd say.

It's a thought I wish I'd never had.

I'm tired of being trapped at home, Dr. Milton, watched every minute. My mother can't even go to work! Listen, I need to get out—I want to see Emmet. You could make that happen.

Emmet and I are not crazy. Maybe we're hybrids, or a new species. We're not something to be medicated back to "normal." When I was fully human—what you would call normal—well, I can barely remember myself then, but I know that everything hurt, and nothing was real. Now, with transformation, everything is real, and except for this foolish boxing in, the pain is gone.

If you try to destroy me and Emmet, the pain that comes back will be my gift to you.

I know how to hunt. I know how to kill.

From: Douglas Bracken <dougman@minimen.com>
To: Dr. Rita I. Milton <Milton@tellet.com>
Sent: Tuesday, November 26—10:22 PM
Subject: Back Stabbers!!!!!!!!

Dr. Milton,

I'm so angry I could puke! I just watched <u>Evening Fling</u>, on Channel 4. Did you see it? It totally sucked! I've lost all respect for Sadie Fuller, even if she does let you see a little bit of her, you know, <u>boobs</u>. Dad says TV reporters these days are nothing more than prostitutes with mics. Except he used another word.

She interviewed Buck Fallow! On TV! As if <u>he</u> knows anything about anything. He even said stuff about me! Like everybody knows I've got the hots for Niki, so it's obvious that what happened is we got porno in the woods, and, in a moment of jealous rage, I "maybe" killed Nicholas Slanger. Huh? THAT DOESN'T MAKE ANY SENSE!!!!!!! Plus it isn't true. How can he say stuff like that? He wasn't even there! Dad already has a call in to a lawyer. I bet Buck was the one who started up the rumors about that whole incest crap, and made the call to Channel 4.

Dr. Milton, everything's going haywire. How can I go back to school after this? I ride the same bus as Buck. Dad says I have to hold my head high and do it, because otherwise the turds win.

You don't believe what Buck said, do you?

I know I should forget everything and go to bed, but I don't sleep well anymore. I keep having freaky dreams about the woods. Animals and woods.

Write me back soon?
Doug
"Rabbits, foxes, snakes, and cats.
At least no spiders, slugs, or rats."

THE FATHER PROJECT

Chapter Eleven

N. sat in Dr. Lee's almost-empty waiting room, flipping through *ITgrrl* magazine. As far as she could figure, it was mostly *TITgrrl* magazine—but what else were Hollywood actresses good for? She smiled. At least with transformation, *all* animals looked great.

She felt a small, pleasant rise of fur on the back of her neck, and gently willed it back down. She'd gotten in a brief run that morning at dawn, dew between her toes.

She flipped another page. Emmet had been with Dr. Lee for twenty-five minutes now. Having a hawk for a brother was getting a bit tedious—he couldn't go anywhere alone anymore. Not since his notorious attack on Jeff Johnson. Not since humanity had begun to seem more and more like an unnecessary option.

Still, this was a pleasant, if chilly, afternoon, and tomorrow was Halloween. A good night for a hunt.

"Is he still in with the doctor?" Her mother, rushing from work, plopped down beside her, out of breath.

N. eyed her mother's lap. Not big and wide, but still inviting. "Yes," she replied. Her mother smoothed N.'s hair back from her forehead—a gesture that, two years ago, would have irritated N.'s twelve-year-old self. Now, a small purr emanated from her throat.

Her mother smiled. "He's been less, I don't know . . . *agitated* or something lately. Don't you agree? And he's been eating better. So I think you were right—he's just a growing boy!"

She picked up a copy of *Mansions* magazine. "I think the dinner on Sunday helped," she continued. "He got to meet Nick. I know it's probably unsettling for the two of you, but it's time we all moved on with our lives."

She flipped a page, so N. flipped one, too. She didn't think her mother would approve of the life she and Emmet were moving on to. And Sunday, Nicholas Slanger had rubbed his leg against hers under the table, then smiled and said, "Excuse me, dear. Didn't mean to bump you." *Ick.* Why were humans so obvious in their deceit? At some point, her mother would have to be alerted to the life *she* was moving on to.

She studied an ITgrrl's swelling bosom, then looked down at her own chest. Well, it didn't matter. She'd be all cat soon enough.

"I've never known a boy to wander off so. Unless I ground him, Emmet's never home during the day." Her mother flipped another page. "He doesn't care about a driver's license, doesn't care about girls. Well, I don't think he likes boys, either. Although it would be okay if he did. I mean, really. I could handle it. I'd love him no matter what." She tucked a strand of hair behind her ear as she focused on an impossibly lush home.

"I wouldn't mind living in that one." Her mother shook her head. "I used to like being where we are, but now—well, there's just something strange about the woods. Maybe we should move." She sighed and turned the page, so N. turned one, too, finding herself confronting more cleavage. "Half the time I think the house is haunted," her mother continued. "I swear I hear things moving around at night. Ghosts, maybe. Wild animals."

N. blinked. She heard all that?

"I saw your brother looking at Melody this past Sunday. She's an eyeful, that one. It's not like he didn't notice."

She's his cousin! N. snarled quietly. How oblivious could her mother be?

Her mother flipped a page and laughed bitterly. "By the way, don't think I haven't tried to find your father this past week and a half. I've talked to everyone. I'm not doing it for me, obviously, but for you and Emmet. You deserve at least that. But I've come up with nothing. I'm beginning to think Mr. Bracken saw someone who just looked like him."

N. pursed her lips. Anything was possible.

Her mother sniffed. "Look at *this* house. Owned by"—she peered at the print—"I don't recognize the name. Some movie star or billionaire, I guess. Who else?" She shook her head.

"Since Mr. Bracken saw—thought he saw—your father near the woods, I even asked Nick if he'd run into him. I showed him a picture. But no. Nothing." She tilted her magazine to look at a huge, flowering garden. "Now, *that's* nice."

"Mrs. Marcona?" The nurse smiled down at them. "Dr. Lee will talk to you now."

Driving home, their mother maintained a stony silence.

Sitting in the back with Emmet, N. discreetly kneaded the edge of the seat, working it with her palms and fingers. Her brother didn't notice. He used to note every cat move she made, laughing silently at their shared secret—but that had been before he'd gotten so close to going over altogether. Increasingly, her catness wasn't of interest to him. She missed the way they used to adventure together, the outdoors a playground for transformation.

She pushed her blunt nails as deeply as possible into the upholstery. For someone who had just been remanded into psychotherapy, Emmet seemed awfully happy, smiling quietly to himself, his eyes focused out the window on the sky. Well, it wasn't that big of a mystery—the doctor hadn't picked up on his real problem at all. Not that, to Emmet, it was a problem. It was his *life*.

She felt her old anger flare, fur prickling heatedly across her skin under her clothes. Claws sprang into small, sharp daggers. She opened her mouth in a silent mewl. Emmet had everything—height, distance, vision. The entire blueness of *above*. What did she have? A few inches between the ground and her nose. Only paws to pad on. What she could see from here.

She was earth. He was sky.

No doctor had remanded *her* into therapy. Was she so terribly invisible? Her situation so unobservable, so uncritical that she didn't also deserve attention? She wanted to reach out and smack Emmet—let him taste claw! A yowl rose in her throat. She'd have his blood! They'd broken their sacred rule once. They could do it again. Her blood would rule!

"It happens all the time to kids of divorce."

N. jerked, startled out of her anger. Her claws retracted, her fur retreated into her skin.

"It's almost a rite of passage these days," her mother continued. "Dad leaves, kids get therapy." Mrs. Marcona smiled brightly in the rearview mirror, trying to cover the tremor in her voice. "So I guess we're right with the program! We'll do the Father Project proud!" Her voice broke, her eyes filling with tears. N. looked away. No doubt a call to Aunt Tam was in order.

They pulled into their driveway, once more locked together in silence. Climbing out, N. stretched, forgetting her anger at Emmet, letting a delicious pleasure travel from her head to her toes. Their sacred rule was safe—for now.

Emmet tore to the front door as their mother pulled the mail out of the box and riffled through it. "Here, Em," she said, entering the house. "Something for you. No return address or name." She smiled crookedly, then her face began to cave. "Maybe I'll go call Aunt Tam." She hurried down the hall.

N. watched Emmet turn the envelope around in his hands, studying it with one eye, then the other. It was a shame she couldn't tell their mother that he didn't need therapy. He merely needed to become what he *was*. Of course, then their mother would need therapy.

She took the envelope from him and slid her finger under the flap. What would happen to their mother once they were fully transformed—and gone? Even if N. could come back and beg for pats and favors, her mother would never know it was her.

N. pulled the card out of the envelope. She didn't like what was in her head: they would end up hurting their mother as much as their father had.

She gulped at the name scrawled across the bottom of the card—

Nicholas Slanger! She felt Emmet lift it from her hand. *"A boy without a father is a sad thing,"* he read, his voice hesitant. *"But strength can come from pain. And so can pleasure. Don't be afraid to be who you are, Emmet. What you are. Don't be afraid to fight the ones who oppress. You ride a fast and brutal wing."*

N. snatched the card back and shoved it into the envelope with trembling fingers. "More crazy talk from Slanger." For sure they'd have to tell their mother something about him, to warn her off—but not yet.

First, they had to figure him out.

From: Douglas Bracken <dougman@minimen.com>
To: Dr. Rita I. Milton <Milton@tellet.com>
Sent: Friday, November 29—11:32 AM
Subject: Mentally Healthless

Dr. Milton,

I'm off for Thanksgiving, except I've got all this homework to do.
Dad really got on my case, as I've failed three quizzes and two tests
since Halloween. I also had a major English paper due this past
Wednesday. But (thanks to Buck Fallow's big fat TV mouth, at least
he's good for <u>something</u>) my English teacher has given me till Monday. He has great faith in me as a student. He's never once written
<u>slumper</u> across the top of my work.

I'm feeling slumpish, though.

I hope you had a good Thanksgiving. Mine was a little depressing.
We went to a buffet over in Harden City, where nobody knows us,
and had restaurant turkey. (Dad refused to drive by the Kitten's
Den. Apparently it's in a different part of town. I kind of wanted to
see it.)

Is there a study somewhere that says that home-cooked turkey
makes people feel better than turkey paid for by the plate? Dad
and Fiona spent the whole time talking about moving--maybe even
to Harden City. He thinks being isolated out here has made it difficult for me. I disagree! I like it out here just fine. Who wouldn't
want to live by the woods? But he's stressed over all the porno talk
going on about me and Niki and Emmet--even though I told him
none of it is true. And he's freaked that Mr. Slanger has disappeared. And that the police found a mysterious bone (which they

still haven't reported on). It's like Dad thinks all this stuff happened because of where we live. But weird things happen everywhere, don't they?

I had another strange dream last night. Niki was walking through the woods (naked! Don't mention that part to anyone, OK?). Anyway, she was trying to tell me something, but I couldn't make out her words. Then a bird flew up from the brush and charged through the trees to the sky. We both watched it leave, then Niki started to cry. I went to touch her, and poof! she was gone. That's it, the whole dream. So--do you think I need psychotherapy or something?

There's one thing I haven't told you, Dr. Milton. Ever since Halloween night, when I ran screaming out of the woods, trying to drag Emmet and Niki along behind me, nothing's been right. Not one single thing. I feel followed all the time. Kind of watched. As if someone's got me under observation. Like I'm an animal at the zoo. Trapped. Weird, huh?

I wonder if, in a psychiatric way, that's what guilt feels like. I mean, if I'd kept my big mouth shut and hadn't called the police, Emmet would have snapped out of his bird stuff, and Niki wouldn't have retreated even further into her cat world.

It's just--have you ever banged your head real hard in the dark, then, half-conscious, tried to round up a snarling, naked girl, who's hissing and scratching at your face, and a full-grown, naked boy, who's all scrunched down on his haunches, flapping his arms and squawking like a crow? It was crazy, Dr. Milton. Maybe it wasn't my fault, but--have you ever messed up real bad on a patient? I feel like I messed up real bad on my two best friends.

And the blood all over their hands and mouths? I think it was their

own. I think they attacked each other. Maybe if I hadn't passed
out, I could have stopped them.

Doug Bracken
"Damned spot not out
Not out
Not
Damn"

Emmet Marcona
Tomington Center—Wing A—Dr. Milton
Assignment
November 30

You're back from Thanksgiving. I confess, I was
lonely. The aides and nurses hardly talked to me
at all. They think I'm too strange. I don't mind the
quiet, but—not hearing your footsteps coming down
the hall reduced my room to more than silence. To
absence. I didn't expect it to bother me so much.

Of course, I had the sky to look at, through my
window.

Mom came to see me last night. She only stayed a
few minutes. I was excited to see her, but she was
tense and unhappy. She didn't hug me. I braced
myself to be touched—I almost wanted it—but it
didn't happen.

Maybe it's just the stress of taking care of Niki. Or
maybe she's finally being honest, admitting to
herself that she doesn't love me. Dr. Milton, I can
forgive her for that. Not everybody in your life can
love you. Please tell her it's okay.

I know that Niki cares about me, even though we're
apart now. I didn't expect to find myself needing

her. But then, I never expected this kind of solitude.

I know you think reading her story is helping me, but in truth it frightens me. I'm trying to cooperate, though, and do what you say.

How can Slanger have touched her? I know it's just a fabrication in her story, but—this upsets me, more than I can say. I want this story to end.

Look, Dr. Milton, I can't protect Niki, or anybody else, if I'm locked up here.

She describes my visit to the doctor. I told Dr. Lee what happened, that I didn't bite Jeff Johnson, but he wanted me to see a psychiatrist. He said I seemed depressed—he was concerned about my isolation.

He didn't understand that being alone is my salvation. Or used to be.

Niki got it right, that Mom was upset, blaming my difficulties on Dad, on the fact that he left. But maybe his leaving opened me up, allowing me to become who I am. What I am. But—

Maybe I really am a hawk! Beak Boy. Dr. Milton, as crazy as that sounds, it would make more sense.

Niki was distressed on that ride home from Dr.

Lee's. She thinks she never gets enough attention, but how can that be true? Dad called her <u>my sweet girl</u>, spent all kinds of time with her. I was never, not even once, his sweet boy.

I told Dr. Lee that I was concerned about Niki, that she missed Dad so much she'd grown dependent on me, but he didn't listen. He said, "I'm concerned about <u>you</u>, Emmet."

But he shouldn't have been. I had the sky. He couldn't see it the way I could, the sky's magnificence, the way it's both close and far away, unattainable. The way it leaves you alone.

Niki—she never knew how to leave me alone. But I accept that. It's how she is.

It's true that I got a second note in the mail from Mr. Slanger. Why did he want my company? I was confused. And I think Niki might have been jealous. Please understand—I never meant to upset her.

There's one thing that Niki doesn't know—that afternoon, after I got Slanger's note, I slipped out of the house, making my way to his place. It was time to confront him on my own terms, in the daylight, not in the dark. But he wasn't there. A piece of paper was taped to his front door, though. <u>Emmet</u>, it said, <u>join me. Freedom will be ours. For the small price of blood. It's only what you want. And deserve.</u>

What did he mean about joining him? Where? Doing what? But he understood my nature. I knew he did! My doubts rushed away, leaving only desire.

I overlooked what he said about blood.

Does Niki know how much I miss her? I mean, not her physical body, not really, but her heart. Wrapped in my blankets at night, before sleep tugs me into darkness, all I think about is her. And then— sometimes—I dream.

You study me, you study Emmet, keeping both of us caged—me at home, Emmet at Tomington. Yes, my mother believes in you; she keeps us contained at your insistence. But why, Milton? Is this your idea of a hunt?

I watch the news when my mother's fallen asleep. Despite all the yapping on TV, no foul play has been determined. And there won't be. A few animal remains could be found—but the police don't understand what to look for. Increasingly, though, I sense that you do. But I bet you won't tell.

Am I right?

Milton Renowned for Work with Teens

by CARL BRENNER
Mid-State News staff writer

GANTON—Dr. Rita I. Milton, known to be working with the two teenagers allegedly responsible for the attack on Nicholas Slanger on Halloween night, has a national reputation for the work she's done with troubled adolescents.

She has published several papers that have appeared in distinguished medical journals, including *The Rocky Mountain Psychiatry Review*. In one article, she described her work with a teenager accused of several murders. While not identified by name, the teen is widely believed to be Johnny Folsom, accused of killing his parents and two siblings. Ultimately found innocent by reason of insanity, he is now confined to a hospital for the mentally insane.

She has worked with a number of other teenagers accused of murder.

Ironically and sadly, her own teenage son, Nathaniel Milton, dis-appeared several years ago, along with his best friend, Eddy Wick. From handwritten notes sent to Dr. Milton, who raised Nathaniel alone, police believe that Eddy Wick probably murdered Milton and hid his body, which has never been found. Wick has also not been seen since.

Some dispute this account, however, noting that Nathaniel Milton was the one with a troubled history, including incidents of cruelty toward animals, and was once arrested for assault. Dr. Milton has never spoken publicly about this incident.

Benny Driscoll, stopping by the Pig Pie for fried chicken and chocolate cake, said, "Just because this big wing-ding doctor works with kids who murder people, that doesn't mean these kids have murdered people. You know what I mean? Everybody needs to take a deep breath and relax."

His girlfriend, Wendy Carwell, disagreed, stating, "In my book, where there's smoke, there's fire. These kids are nuts."

THE FATHER PROJECT

Chapter Twelve

"Well," said N.'s mother, eyeing the three of them nervously. Her pointed black hat slid over one ear and she righted it, only to have it slip over the other. "Stupid costume." She smoothed her long black dress and shrugged the matching cape, with its shiny purple lining, over her shoulders. The hat tumbled forward. "Oh, for Pete's sake."

"You look great, Mom," N. ventured. Anything to get her out the door.

"Yeah, you look terrific!" Doug chimed in, holding a plastic bag behind his back.

"Are you *sure* you won't come to Aunt Tam's Halloween party? I feel funny going by myself. Lots of people will be there—all her neighbors—and I'm sure other kids will show up." Her hat avalanched again, and she rammed it down over both ears. "And, of course, Melody."

N. hissed quietly.

"Doug, you're more than welcome to come along. We can call your father—"

"He's on his way to pick up Fiona. They're going to the B-Grade to see *Swordo's Sheath*." He grinned at N. "They're having a Halloween special, on top of the He-Man popcorn special. Everyone's supposed to wear a costume. The best one gets a free season pass. Dad's going as a pirate."

"Really?" Mrs. Marcona looked puzzled. "I thought the B-Grade only showed old X-ra—oh, never mind." She took the broom Emmet silently handed her. "So, you've got your own movies picked out?"

Doug opened his bag and peeked. "*Mudsucker Death #3*, and *Killer's Romp in Paradise*." He looked at Mrs. Marcona. "They're both PG-13."

"Well, all right. Emmet, you're in charge. Keep the doors locked, now. We never get any trick-or-treaters this far out, so you won't have to worry about that. There are snacks and stuff in the kitchen." She smiled weakly. "I wish Nick had been able to come."

"Maybe you'll meet a hunky werewolf," Doug suggested. "Dad says the heart is a lonely hunter only until it finds someone to hunt with."

Her lips twitched. "Well, I guess that makes a certain, um, sense." She held on to her hat. "I'm off, then. You have Aunt Tam's number. I won't be late."

They stood at the door and waved until she pulled away.

"Okay," said N. "How long does it take to get to the clearing?"

"I've never done it in the dark before, so"—Doug synchronized his watch with N.'s—" we'd better leave by 8:15 at the latest. It's only 7:23." He looked at her, his eyes bright with hope. "Maybe we can eat something?"

She didn't think he'd be interested in the raw pork chops sitting in the refrigerator. "We've got some frozen Pizza-Petes, and tons of chips."

"Great!"

They trooped to the kitchen.

N. had never really ventured into the woods before at night. It was hard to get out when her mother was home, which was almost always. And when she was gone, there was Emmet to worry about. She pulled her shirt collar closer as the chilly air invaded her pullover—despite her love of the dark, maybe she also feared it a bit.

She was still part human.

Getting Emmet out the door hadn't been easy. It had finally come down to Doug pulling and N. pushing. Now they walked, linked hand in hand, like little kids—touch evidently better for Emmet than terror. Doug led, pointing his flashlight with his free hand. Emmet took the middle. N. came behind, her flashlight a pale follow-up. Both beams bobbed like small, flaming torches, casting an eerie light into the woods.

The moon shone naked in the sky.

They walked and walked, pushing branches aside, then dodging them when they whipped back—the cold, feral night turning their nervousness to fear. What was that? Just a twig, breaking. The black trees they passed beneath hovered like lonely, bitter wraiths. And that? A branch grabbed her pullover and N.'s heart leapt, sending blood shrieking through her veins. Wait—that? Just a tiny animal scurrying away, frightened by such heavy-footed, unwelcome guests, its small sound magnified by fear. What sort of noise would a larger animal make?

What hunted hawk—or cat?

She wanted to slink close to the earth, her body blending with the ground, her paws carefully finding their way, her whiskers warning of what was close. She wanted to meld with the dark until it frightened her no more. Tension would mount as danger approached. Muscles easing would tell when it had passed. She wanted that instinct, that sureness—but this, so far, was a human journey.

Emmet's hand gripped hers like a talon. For all she knew, his eyes were shut.

They walked and walked.

The trees seemed to finally step back, providing a small, moonlit space.

"This is it," said Doug, flicking the beam from his flashlight around the empty clearing. "I guess Mr. Slanger isn't here yet. There's a log we can sit on, if you want, and—"

"So, you made it."

They turned, startled, as Slanger, tall and lean, stepped into the clearing, his hair gleaming in the moon's glow, his smile the dark underside of light.

N. could feel Emmet trembling. She squeezed his hand harder, willing him courage.

"Welcome, Emmet," said Slanger. "I hoped you'd come. And you've brought company. Good." He ran his eyes over N., and her heart shrank to a small, hard knot in her chest. He smiled again at Emmet. "It's time to be what you truly are."

N. watched as Emmet, his eyes fixed on Slanger, nodded.

"I've seen your true self, Emmet," Slanger said. "I've watched you in the woods. But you've known that, haven't you? And enjoyed the attention." He chuckled.

"What do you want?" N. demanded, swallowing her fright.

"Why, everything, of course. Your life. Your soul. I'm a creator of stories, in need of characters. What else would I want?"

"I *knew* it." Doug stepped forward. "This is all just stuff for your next book, isn't it? Using local kids with problems to spice up a novel—"

"What makes you think I'm the one using them?" Slanger's laugh was as cold as the night. "Whose story do you think this is?"

"That's crazy talk," Doug huffed. "Words that don't make any sense!"

Siss-s-s-s. Siss-s-s-s. What was that? N. tensed, looking around.

"Oh, but they do." Slanger stroked his chin. "All of us are prey in someone else's hunt, our passions linked irrevocably to someone else's pain. We take what we need. Especially artists like myself."

Siss-s-s-s. Siss-s-s-s.

"Oh—art, fart," snorted Doug.

What hunted hawk? What hunted cat? N.'s muscles bunched to the point of pain. What creature crept about?

Emmet's eyes shone, newly strange and confident. Alarmed, N. silently mewled, *danger* singing through her bones. Her spine stretched, easing her into the strength of sinew, the blade of claw.

Slanger slowly reached into his jacket. "Yes, art." He smiled gently. "You see, Niki, art creates, but love destroys. Your father is proof."

"What?" N. bristled. "What about my father?"

"Look out!" Doug yelled. "He's got a knife!"

N. leapt, a perfect arc, lithe muscles propelling her through the air, leaving what was human behind, clothes fallen to the ground. By the time she reached Slanger, she was cat, claws unsheathed, teeth bared.

Something glittered on the ground. But Slanger was gone!

She twisted desperately in midair, pulling in her feet, crash-landing upright on the leaf-damp ground. Ears back, tail fat, she growled a warning, then howled in frustration.

Footsteps thudded away. Whipping her head, she saw Doug tearing back through the woods. She cringed as he whacked his head on a limb and fell to the ground like a squash.

Siss-s-s-s. Siss-s-s-s. What stalked?

Emmet!

He bore down shrieking, beak harsh, wings steel, talons sharp. She dove for cover behind the log.

Siss-s-s-s. Siss-s-s-s.

Tearing out, she took the clearing, Slanger's long, impossibly thin shape following, a bright, cold hatred in his eyes.

He was snake! He hunted cat and hawk!

Emmet! she cried as she stumbled, her cat's grace gone. *Help!*

Emmet sank to the log and folded his wings, content to watch.

She froze, panicked. Where to run? Slanger was close. No choice but one, she crouched and pushed, a living rock. Target hit, she tore Emmet's feathers, dug with claw.

His shriek was hers as they thrashed, rolling across the forest floor, fur matted with leaves, mashed with wings, both dampened with blood.

Her jaws clamped down, flesh found.

Something flickered and gleamed. She paused.

It was Emmet's own eye, gold in the moonlight, blank with a bird's cold lust—to hunt and mate—humanity gone.

He wanted her dead; she wanted his blood. Yet hadn't they, in their human life, known love? She held him tight, giddy, rushed—should she save him or thrust?

She let go; he flapped free; Slanger struck from the rear, a black rope twisting, a noose encroaching. He gripped her gut, encircling her neck, squeezing her lungs.

Choking, helpless, she slumped. Emmet dove, piercing her side, struggling aloft, hauling them both, the three of them bound.

Doug! she cried. Breath lost, she peered as she rose, looking downward through trees and leaves and brush. There he was! No, it was only his clothes, empty and slack, spread on the ground. He was gone.

Emmet's grip failed. Tumbling, slipping, she plunged toward the earth, as air, sweet and cold, quickened her lungs. Slanger fell, a harsh rope, a black, snapping whip.

She hit something soft. Scrambling upright, rolling off, she quickly saw what: Her cushion a rabbit, dead or shocked.

Where was the snake? Rebounded to life, bloodied and torn, she flexed her claws.

Siss-s-s-s. Siss-s-s-s. He slithered forward, unfazed by his fall. She lashed as he struck. Her brother bore down, beak wide, talons sharp—

Help! she yowled. Would no one come? *Help!* she shrieked.

Something leapt in the dark—what beast was this?—and snagged her brother, pulling him down. N. pounced as he fell, sinking her claws. Emmet's wings struggled upward, they fought in the air, N. twisting and shrieking, determined to kill. They tumbled back down, his blood on her tongue.

Springing aside, she panted, exhausted. Emmet bore up, but the new beast jumped, Emmet's neck in its mouth. N. yowled, hot with lust. He was hers to kill.

Emmet fell once again, and the beast stood clear.

The black cat who had sat in her yard.

Every hair on her body bolted upright. The black cat who'd eaten the head off a squirrel! Far bigger than she, it flicked its tail slowly. Stunned, N. saw who it was.

Her father, transformed. Come back to save her. Home, all along.

Joy leapt in her blood, unbearable tension alive in her limbs, wet flooding her mouth. He loved her, he did! This was the hunt—her father and her, killing snake and hawk!

Up rose Slanger. N. shrieked a warning, but her father was fast. He bit and slashed, springing sideways, then around to strike back, sinking tooth-blade and claw. She jumped in and tore, leather skin in her mouth. They rolled on the ground, the three of them straining, N.'s muscles now breaking, beginning to fail. Harder, she snarled. Bite deeper, claw sharper! Blood scented her nose. *Dig, rip, and claw!*

But Slanger was strong. Her father panted, betraying his age, silenced by pain. Blood flowed from his mouth. Slanger squeezed tighter, his eyes shining bright.

Emmet plunged from the sky. N. jerked as the snake was torn from her fur, her father released, falling heavy and limp. She yowled in despair.

Emmet bore the snake up, tearing its flesh with his beak and claw. Slanger fell, bleeding hard, broken and spent. He shuddered and stopped. Emmet flew down, tired but triumphant, as if he had won.

She tensed her legs, prepared to fight. But he merely landed, perched on the log, beak open and panting, settling his wings.

N. scrambled upright. Her brother stayed calm. Their fight was done. She turned to her father. Her truest mate! He'd come back to save her. He'd never left home.

And now he was gone.

Dried leaves rustled. She turned her head.

A fox stepped out. It eyed them, the moon's bright gleam in its eye, and quickly began to transform—front limbs into arms, back limbs into legs, its shape growing tall, with a now human stride.

A woman of beauty, caught in the moonlight, her hair deeply red, stood laughing before them. Naked, she panted, her eyes dark and wild.

"Thank you," she said. "You've done what I wanted." Her sly, jesting laugh pricked the chilly air. "Slanger wanted to trap me, enslave my soul to his useless art. Your father, who mistook our passion for love, wanted me, too. Their jealousy clashed. But no man can rule me, and now they're both dead. Dominion is mine!"

Transforming to fox, she barked and was gone.

Emmet Marcona
Tomington Center—Wing A—Dr. Milton
Assignment
December 1

Niki got it wrong! Yes, we fought—but not like that!
Not as animals.

And Dad wasn't there. Not as a cat. Not as
anything!

He couldn't have been.

We fought because Slanger urged me to go away
with him. He understood my heart, what I needed
to survive. I was invisible to my father, but Slanger—
he saw me! And he knew that staying at home,
staying with Niki, would kill me. He understood what
family can do, how it can make you deny who you
are.

I went to the clearing like he asked. It was hard. It
was dark. I was so frightened! I wanted to go home
and be safe, but I knew that Slanger was right; it
was time for me to become who I am, and if he
could help me—

I didn't know that Slanger would betray me. I
thought he cared about me, Dr. Milton. I thought he
would help me leave and find my way. But he
handed me a knife. I stood there, confused.

There was no black cat, no snake. Niki's mad! But how can I blame her? She tried to take the knife away. She struggled to keep me, pull me back, make me love only her—for a moment, I thought I had to kill her to be free.

But I didn't, Dr. Milton.

I only pricked, I only drew a little blood. I came to my senses. Doesn't that count for anything?

If anyone died, it wasn't then. It wasn't by my hand.

But what you've told me today is a lie. It isn't true. Why have you come with such a crazy tale? I trusted you! Niki never held that knife. Not Halloween night. Not ever. She didn't kill our father. He never touched her. She never touched me. Yes, we lured him into the woods, those two long years ago—but only to talk to him alone, away from our mother. We begged him to stay. We fought, but only with words. And we lost. He went away. We never saw him again.

We never told Mom. How could we explain?

I don't know where Slanger has gone. He saw I couldn't leave, that I had no will, could not fight for who I was, could not separate from my sister. Disgusted, he took the knife and left.

Dr. Milton, despite your lies, you're all I have. I feel dizzy, weak. Something flutters in my chest, I can barely hold this pen. As if my mind has already tried to flee, transform into wings.

You see, she was there—the woman I dreamed of, with dark red hair. The one who held a bird at her wrist.

Niki and I fought, then parted, exhausted. And this woman stepped into the clearing. For a moment, I thought she was Niki, all grown up. And seeing her, naked, unashamed—I'm embarrassed to tell, but it's true—I knew she was my true and only mate. She had to be! Who else could claim my body? Who else could will my soul? Not Slanger, that teller of lies. My solitude, my sojourn in confusion, had merely been a preparation for our bond. Together we'd own both woods and sky.

Niki and I are mates! She cannot fly, any more than I can stalk my prey on the ground. But her paws will pad the forest, her mouth will cry my name. And me?

I am hawk! I rule the sky! The forest below is mine.

From: Douglas Bracken <dougman@minimen.com>
To: Dr. Rita I. Milton <Milton@tellet.com>
Sent: Monday, December 02—3:24 PM
Subject: Re: Last Night's Dream

Dr. Milton,

How did you guess I had another weird dream?

I was walking through the woods (this is the dream) and saw a fox.
(I see a fox every so often in real life.) (In the woods, I mean. Not
like on the school bus or in the grocery store.)

Anyway, in my dream last night, the fox turned into you! Except
I've never seen you, of course. (So how did I know it was you? I
did, though. Weird, huh?) Are foxes supposed to be wise? It could
be symbolic or something, since you're a psychiatrist.

A bird was in the dream, too, like the one I dreamed about when
Niki was naked. (!) A hawk or raven of some kind. Anyway, in my
dream, you had trapped it in some kind of box. You could have let
it out, but you didn't. (You were kind of mean.) (Sorry.)

It's strange that I've been talking to you so much, and we've never
met. Maybe I could catch a ride with Mrs. Marcona some time and
come see you at Tomington. And I'd really like to visit with Emmet.

Any word on that bone in the woods?

Doug Bracken
 "Dr. Freud once spied a fox
 Who kept a raven in a box.

'Ve must analyze dis case,
But first our hungers ve'll erase
By eating Wiener schnitzel, lots.'"

(We're having hot dogs and sauerkraut for dinner, with mustard.
Sauerkraut is a vegetable, isn't it?)

You've been downstairs talking with my mother for over an hour, Milton. What are you saying? Why is she crying? And why are the police and an ambulance pulling up in front of my house?

Don't try to trick me. I know who you are. Because of my blood, because of these woods, I transform. Like you, I'm not one, but two—human and beast. And like you, I'm a teller of lies. Which one of me will you hunt? Which one of me will you kill?

Don't think that this story is done. There are all kinds of endings, happy or sad—but there's only one truth. You cannot silence the teller of tales. I'll escape and survive, and Emmet will, too.

This story goes on. I'll scratch it on the walls, I'll write it out in blood. The way it ends is up to you.

Second Teen Hospitalized

by Carl Brenner
Mid-State News staff writer

GANTON—In a dramatic development, the girl believed to be one of the teenagers who allegedly attacked Nicholas Slanger has been admitted to the Tomington Center for Psychiatric Disorders. Her brother, another alleged attacker, is already receiving treatment there. Both are in locked security wings.

Calls to the girl's home went unanswered, as did calls placed to the Tomington Center, and to Dr. Rita I. Milton, who is treating both children. Dr. Milton specializes in the treatment of adolescents who have committed murder. As a teenager, her own son, Nathaniel Milton, was either the victim of murder himself, or, as some believe, the perpetrator of the murder of his best friend, Eddy Wick. Both boys remain missing.

At a recent press conference, Chief Wilkinson refused to confirm or deny reports that murder charges are about to be brought against the two teenagers, or that a murder weapon had been found.

Tammy Burton, eating the roast beef special at the Pig Pie, said, "If they *did* kill Slanger, they're sick and need treatment, not prison." Her companion, Hilton Tubb, disagreed. "Hang 'em," he said.

If these teenagers are indeed charged with murder, Dr. Milton will once more find herself at the center of a storm of death and destruction.

THE FATHER PROJECT

The End

N. stood in the clearing, becoming aware of her girl's body once more. The wounds from the fight, grown small, prickled and burned. In the moon-touched dark, she hurriedly searched for jeans and shirt and pullover, shrugging them on.

Emmet, too, got dressed. N. watched as the rabbit she'd landed on, cushioning her fall from the sky, transformed—growing to human size, turning into Doug. Astonished, he stared at his hands, then looked around wildly, shocked—and dove for his clothes.

N. picked up a flashlight and flicked it on. The snake that was Slanger didn't move; nor did the black cat.

Her father was dead. He'd fought the snake to save her life, and lost his own. Is that what a father was? Someone who gave his life for yours? Who finally came home? Who loved you, no matter what? Human, she couldn't read her heart.

Something glinted on the ground—she reached to pick it up. A knife. So Slanger had meant to kill them all, to bend them to his rule. Did the fox intend that, too?

"What happened?" Doug groaned, rubbing his head.

"You knocked yourself out." She slipped the knife into her pocket.

"Then took off my clothes and turned into some kind of crazy Halloween rabbit? I don't think so."

N. smiled quietly. He'd wakened to the spell of the woods, encouraged, perhaps, by the blood they had shared when they'd broken the glass in her kitchen. But he was far too human still; he'd never completely transform, or understand. Best to leave it alone. "I think you imagined that part."

He sniffed. "Maybe I hallucinated or something. But I didn't imagine being naked. And now I'm *freezing*." N. reached to the ground and handed him his jacket. "What happened to Slanger, anyway?" he asked.

N. shrugged. No point in showing him the bodies; he wouldn't believe the truth. "He went home. You were right about him wanting to use us in his story. But we didn't cooperate."

"I'd like to put *him* in a book, and see how he likes it." Doug searched the pockets of his jacket. "Hey, I found a Snickers!"

Emmet didn't move. "I dreamed that we—" He stopped, uncertain, doubt clouding his eyes.

"You didn't dream anything," N. said. "It's late and you're tired. Let's go home."

They followed the path back through the woods.

"That candy bar wasn't enough," Doug complained, breaking their silence. "I'm still hungry. Which might be why my head still hurts. The Pig Pie makes great apple fritters. They serve them hot, with or without vanilla ice cream. I wish we could go get some."

"Your head hurts because you banged it on a tree limb." *And then got clobbered by a falling cat*, N. didn't add. She aimed her flashlight at her watch. "And the Pig Pie is closed." She paused. "Halloween is almost over."

"Is it too late to make some more Pizza-Petes?"

Something scampered by in the woods. N. whirled, waving her flashlight, catching something streaking away, short and dark and long—a weasel? Then there was nothing.

Just night. And darkness. And death.

And a fox who ruled.

She shuddered. What perversity would this fox visit upon them? Slanger—well, no need now to warn their mother about Slanger.

And their father—N.'s heart constricted like a fist. Her father.

He'd been trapped by a woman who was cruel, and had learned a harsh truth—one you could read in one of his columns, if you wanted to look them up. N. had a bunch stashed away in a drawer. Like the one where he'd interviewed that famous psychiatrist who treated troubled adolescents. N., fascinated, had memorized her words.

"We all struggle for dominance, each in our own way—even mothers over their own children—acting out our private dramas, our psychosexual traumas. But some—those with terribly wounded psyches, bearing deep emotional scars—go too far. For them, there is no compassion for others; a consuming grandiosity rules. The lust for power becomes its own end, and passion is merely a game to be played. I know something about that on a personal level. I lost my own son to someone else's sickness."

Really? And just whose sickness was that? Who was the true destroyer?

Pausing once, watching Emmet and Doug continue their walk on the narrow path that traversed the woods, N. slipped away. She had prey to hunt.

Hi! Last night was just so weird. My head still hurts, a little. But it's great we all got to stay home from school today ... how'd we manage that?? :D

Dad called in sick, which he never does, so he's home today, too. But he's not sick ... he's happy! (And v tired.) He says an occasional mental health day is good for all of us. (!!)

Fiona said she'd get married! They didn't win the B-Grade contest or anything, even though Fiona went as Little Bo Peep ... but Dad says he won <u>her</u>! He was so excited he couldn't stop talking. We didn't get to bed till, like, 3:30.

Then I had the weirdest dream ... I think it was a dream. Anyway, my mother came and sat at the foot of my bed ... she looked just like she did the last time she came, quiet and smiling. She said, "Tell Dad I'm happy for him." That was it. Then I woke up--if I was really asleep, I mean--so I decided to wake Dad up, too, and tell him what happened. He started to cry, which freaked me out, so I went back to bed. This morning, though, he was OK and made us waffles for breakfast--except it was noon, so I guess that was lunch.

We're having Hawaiian hamburgers for dinner ... Dad's lighting up the grill. A cookout on the first day of November! (By the way, did you know that yesterday was Keats's birthday? October 31. A v famous poet.)

Speaking of poets, I finished my poem. Here's the rest of it:

On Halloween night Dad went to the B-Grade
Dressed as a pirate, his date as Bo-Peep.
<u>Swordo's Sheath</u> was playing, the He-Man popcorn tasted
   great.
"Fiona," Dad said, "let's do this for keeps.
It's obvious, like Swordo, for love we were made."
Fiona said, "You are my only sheep."

So it's true--they're engaged to be married.
This means I'll have a stepmother, which I hope isn't bad.
They want the reception at the Pig Pie, then she'll be carried
Across our doorstep in her wedding dress, by Dad,
Who might need to work out ahead of time, so he can still
   stand once she's ferried.
This ends "The Ballad of Fiona and Dad."

Do u think it's okay that I used "Dad" twice as a rhyme? He is a main part of the poem. Did u ever write anything of yr own for the Father Project? It's due next week.

Doug

P.S. What really happened last night?

Sitting in front of her computer, N. examined the knife she'd found in the woods, then dropped it into the trash. She had no use for such weapons.

She closed out her e-mail, then stood up. Reaching her arms over her head, she stretched a delicious stretch from the tips of her fingers to the tips of her toes. Her fingernails sharpened slightly, then retracted. Her bed looked overwhelmingly comfy. All she needed was a warm body to provide heat. Maybe Emmet—

No. He was tired and confused. She'd leave him alone.

She climbed on her bed, pushing her quilt and pillows around until she found a perfect circle of comfort, then curled up into a ball. She purred, her mind going pleasantly blank and gray, then wonderfully black.

She shot upright, blinking and looking around her room. Why was she in bed? She stared at the clock. It was nearly six—dinnertime! She'd slept for an hour.

She rolled off her bed and went to pull the shade against the already black night. Behind the house stretched the woods, dark and eternal.

Who really ruled? She refocused her eyes. The window reflected back a fourteen-year-old girl with blue eyes and red-gold hair. Not exactly pretty, not exactly plain.

Human.

For now.

From:	Douglas Bracken <dougman@minimen.com>
To:	Dr. Rita I. Milton <Milton@tellet.com>
Sent:	Wednesday, December 04—10:44 PM
Subject:	Sad and Lonely

Dear Dr. Milton,

It's hard for me to write to you now. I'm pretty upset about Niki. I can't stand to think of her locked up in a hospital. And that murder charge is crap! I'm glad Mrs. Marcona is hiring a good lawyer.

It's funny, but you never told me if you're related to John Milton. I mean, I know it doesn't matter. And I know I got pretty obnoxious this afternoon. I'm sorry I called you a b****, especially after you'd come all the way out to the house to talk to me in person. I'm not supposed to use language like that. Thanks for saying you won't tell Dad. I was just, you know, upset about Niki and Emmet. They're my friends.

Dad says I can't see them anymore, even if everything turns out OK and no murder charges are brought and they stop being crazy. I don't know if I can obey him, though. I think they need a friend now more than ever.

It's strange that your hair turned out to be the same color as it was in my dream--red. Darker than Niki's. Has she given you a hard time about that? I think she's a little vain about her hair color. She likes to be unique. I guess that's how I'd describe her, if I had to. Unique.

I'm sorry a patient attacked you and scratched your face. I'm really glad it wasn't Niki or Emmet. They're in enough trouble already. It sounds like your eye will be OK, though--and the eye patch doesn't look bad at all. I didn't realize the violence that surrounded your work.

I was surprised when you told me that Tomington Associates wants to buy Mr. Slanger's property. Once (if) he's officially pronounced dead, that is. I didn't know you were the president of a psychiatric group. You're probably right, though, that it would be a good location for a private hospital. And I bet if the place was really spruced up, you could get a lot of rich patients.

Maybe Emmet and Niki could stay there? They're not rich, but the Tomington Center is so far away. We could be neighbors again! If I don't relocate, that is. I'm hoping Dad and Fiona will change their minds about moving. I have some reason to be optimistic, as I overheard Dad admit to Fiona that he likes being close to the woods. He loves it when deer come into the backyard--good thing we don't have a vegetable patch!--plus I still wash dishes at the Pig Pie on Saturdays, and how would I get to work? I won't have my license for another year, and it's not like they want to chauffeur me around all the time.

So--do Niki and Emmet know about the bone yet? I mean, that it might be their father's? You seemed sure, but on the news tonight Chief Wilkinson said the tests were inconclusive, so maybe it's somebody else's.

If the bone is Mr. Marcona's, though--well, I know that neither Niki nor Em had anything to do with it. With it getting there, I mean. You know, like in killing him. They missed him something terrible, and I don't think you go around killing someone you love. Even if he is about to abandon you. I know you said (OK, this is the part where I yelled at you--sorry) that when siblings, you know, do stuff together, stuff they shouldn't be doing, that sometimes it's because they have a weird relationship with their parents--but don't we all? Not abusive, I mean. Just--well, have you ever met my dad? I love him a lot, but he is a little strange.

I don't believe porno stuff was going on among any of them.

And Niki as a murderer? Well, that's the second time I called you a name. Sorry.

They're okay, Dr. Milton. Maybe if I hadn't been such a major dope, running into a tree, I could tell you exactly what happened on Halloween night. But I only know the aftermath--Niki and Emmet covered with blood, naked and crazy. Please don't think the worst of them. Things happen in the dark that you don't expect. And the only animal involved was me, being a dodo.

I just know that Niki and Emmet are innocent. But now even you're saying they aren't. I'll be honest, Dr. Milton (I've read that honesty is both a poet's lance and shield), I don't believe you anymore.

I have to go to bed now. Maybe I'll dream about my mother--she'll smile at me, and tell me everything will be all right. I'd like that.

Doug Bracken
"Though 'The Beginning'
Turns into 'The End,'
I'm not a stinky slumper,
I'm sticking by my friends."

Emmet Marcona
Tomington Center—Wing A—Dr. Milton
Assignment
December 5

Yes, the new medication has calmed me down. I
don't feel so—agitated. I was able to finish Niki's
story.

You say they found Dad's bone in the woods, but
that's fiction. Just like all of this—fiction.

Poor Niki. To her, Dad will always be coming back,
always returning.

She wanted a happy ending. She wrote one: Dad
never hurt her—he saved her life. Came back and
saved her life. She doesn't even see what's there
to see in her own words, her own story—that I am
the one who finally destroyed Slanger, who saved
her life and her heart.

Like Dad, she gives me no credit.

He was a selfish man, Dr. Milton. He would never
have given up his freedom, not for her, not for any
of us.

Maybe he deserved to die. But Niki didn't kill him.

She's here now, isn't she, locked up on Wing C. A
prisoner, just like me. Are you giving her pills, too, to
make her madness go away?

This is what you say you believe—that she and Dad were improperly close; that, jealous over his affair with another woman, wanting him for herself, she murdered him in revenge. She then turned to me, beguiling and seducing me so I wouldn't tell.

That isn't true. None of it. Our father left us, yes, but we let him go. We had to. He didn't want to stay.

You want me to betray Niki, to say she also murdered Slanger, because he wanted me to leave and she refused to give me up. It would be a neat and tidy ending to this twinned insanity you say we share, our crazy bid to shield our past, to hide our guilt and shame. You could write us up, couldn't you? A story of your own. One that would make you famous, as a teller of sick tales, a teller of lies. But that's a price I will not pay, not even for freedom. It's true that I can't bear this captivity much longer, but I will not lie for you.

I've got that fluttering in my chest again—like a frightened bird trying to escape. Before, your words would calm me, but now they only bring me dread. I wish I could fly away. Leave this room. Leave you. Slip out on the wind, and be free.

That's all I've ever wanted—to leave the prison that contained me, the sadness of our home. Niki understood that about me. Maybe that's our greatest tie.

It's true she was obsessed with touch. And yes, I wanted her to leave me alone. She didn't. Still, we were bound.

In my dream, the one I told you about, a fox turned into a beautiful woman with red hair. She held me in her hands, a frightened bird, then released me to the sky.

Who did that for me, Dr. Milton? I know it wasn't you.

Was it Niki, finally giving me my freedom, giving me my life?

You say I'm trapped only by the cage of insanity, yet you are the one who locks me in. You have no love for me at all, you'll never let me go.

Niki—dear sister, holder of my heart—listen to these words.

I know you're close, a few hallways and locked doors away. We're prisoners now together. With your cat's ears, can you hear me crying through these walls? I need your touch, your warmth, the way you give me substance. Tonight, before you sleep, whisper a story. Write it on the walls. Write it out in blood. Give me life. Give me wings.

<u>Please.</u>

Niki Marcona
Tomington Center—Wing C—Dr. Milton
Assignment
December 6

Do you like prophecy, Milton? Then you'll
enjoy this.
Tell Emmet he'll soon be free. You've kept us
penned and separated far too long.
   Part of this story has already happened—
ha ha!—some of it is yet to come true. So
watch your back!
   You can't rule by locking me up. You can
cage Emmet—he's timid at heart—but no key
can keep me in.
   By the way, who scratched your face? The
eye patch is rather becoming. You look like a
pirate.
   Meow.

Slanger Spotted?

by CARL BRENNER
Mid-State News staff writer

GANTON—A man has reportedly spotted Nicholas Slanger at a crowded resort in France.

Speaking through an interpreter, Claude Jean-Paul, a longtime fan of Slanger's work (which has been translated into several languages), said he spotted the elusive writer, along with a female companion, slipping into a villa in the south of France.

"I'm a big fan," said Jean-Paul. "It's definitely him. If he uses this Halloween stuff in his next book, it's going to be *huge!*" No one else has confirmed the sighting.

If true, it lends credence to the theory proposed by Hank Cuff, a regular at the Pig Pie Diner, that this has all been a hoax. "The guy's a nutcase," he said. "And probably that doctor, too. Didn't she treat him at one time? I bet they're in this together."

No one else sitting at the Pig Pie counter agreed with Mr. Cuff.

In other developments, while an unnamed source has said that the bone found in the woods is definitely that of the teenagers' father, authorities refuse to confirm or deny that report. Experts outside the case have speculated that the condition of the bone may be too deteriorated to make a positive match.

Also, police have still not located a knife believed to be a possible murder weapon, nor traced such a weapon to any specific individual.

In the end, this case may be one that only a psychiatrist can figure out.

THE FATHER PROJECT

The True End

Eyes round, ears upright, the cat crouched on the ground, muscles tight. Nothing moved, no sound intrigued. Cat hunted fox.

She padded over the leaf-thick mulch, slinking through the moonlit night.

Increasing her pace—ignoring pain, ignoring the blood—she padded on.

There! Ahead in the dark, slinking through brush, too far yet to snare, the fox paused, lifting one foot, raising its snout. It sniffed the air. The cat froze, becoming stone. The fox moved on.

Scent flowered and bloomed. Damp earth and brittle leaves teased the cat's senses, igniting her lust—the moon a bright beacon glinting above. Mouth wet with longing, she mewled without sound. What greater desire than to run through the night, wildness upon her. To do this forever!

The trail stretched on.

Limping, tired, out of breath, still tracking the fox, she fought the chill. The fur that had always kept her warm lay matted and damp—strength seeped from her heart.

Her eyes drooped shut as she gradually slowed, picking her way. She paused, trembling, close to collapse. Perhaps sleep would come. Tomorrow she'd hunt, her heart relaxed, her muscles fresh. If she turned back now, joining her brother, joining their friend, heading home in the dark—

The animal hit, her scruff in its jaws. She shrieked and clawed, but found only air. Tossed back and forth, clamped by the fox, her neck almost cracked, she spit and yowled. A furious shake, and she flew from its mouth.

The fox yipped and howled. The cat sprang, finding target, and rode its back. Digging with claw, she clung and yowled while the fox bucked and danced, yelping with pain. In a final surge, she flung herself forward, rear claws into back, front claws into face, raking an eye.

The fox screamed and shook, flinging the cat. Bleeding, hurt, the fox ran.

The cat shrieked, triumphant. She tore through the woods in determined pursuit, joy muffling her pain and stanching her blood. The hunt was on!

The sun—determined to end the dark—pushed itself up. The cat finally halted—drooping, exhausted, panting hard. She stared at the long black asphalt road, watching taillights depart. This road led toward town, and then beyond. From just too far, she'd seen the fox, saw it transform—saw the weasel, too, take its shape as a man—then heard the car doors open and shut, the engine turned on. Now the acrid scent of gasoline burned.

The cat paused a moment, the asphalt hard. She knew who the fox was, the weasel, too, and what they had wrought.

Fur matted with blood, pads bruised and torn, the cat limped on, following the edge of the silent road. It would take a while to track them down, but she'd get the fox and her bastard son. Her brother was waiting. He needed her touch. She needed his heart.

She silently mewled, gaining strength as she walked.

Lying in bed, the girl blinked awake. The small, darkened room, foreign and strange, admitted no hope. Tired, bruised—how long had she been here, apart from her brother, apart from the woods, alone with her pain?

She tensed as the door clicked open, dim light flooding in—the night nurse making his rounds. He looked like a weasel. Pretending sleep, she closed her eyes. He turned to leave.

Now!

Transformed into cat, shedding her gown, she scooted behind him, just at his heels, making no sound.

She was out!

Crouching, tensed, she hid in the open, a small, silent stone. He relocked her door; she followed him down the linoleum hall—he didn't see her or hear. Passing a fountain set in the wall, she ducked into its recess; he continued his rounds.

His footsteps finally disappeared, and she poked her head out— muscles tight, whiskers sleek, twin ears cocked. She would follow the sound she had heard all day, passing through walls like a keening ghost—her brother, crying her name.

Shoes clicked down the hall. She darted back, scrunching down, freezing in place. Tucked in the recess, she silently hissed at the ankles that passed—the woman's own! Darting out, keeping close, slinking low, she followed behind, knowing where she'd end up—at another door, a locked room, her brother inside. Shadowing her foe, she'd quickly get in. Then Emmet would fly, his talons sharp, and she would yowl. They were mated for life, their purpose clear.

Corner the fox. Kill.

DATE DUE